SCHOOL EDITION

A BOY NAMED
Ossie

CLASSIC JAMAICAN CHILDHOOD STORIES

I0608527

Earl Mckenzie

LMH PUBLISHING LIMITED

Editor: K. Sean Harris
Cover Image: Earl McKenzie (a copy of his original painting)
Cover Design: Sanya Dockery
Book Design, Layout & Typesetting: Sanya Dockery

Published by LMH Publishing Limited
Suite 10-11, Sagicor Industrial Park
7 Norman Road
Kingston C.S.O., Jamaica
Tel.: (876) 938-0005; 938-0712
Fax: (876) 759-8752
Email: lmhbookpublishing@cwjamaica.com
Website: www.lmhpublishing.com

Printed in the U.S.A.   ISBN: 978-976-8245-65-6

NATIONAL LIBRARY OF JAMAICA CATALOGUING-IN-PUBLICATION DATA

McKenzie, Earl
    A boy named Ossie : classic Jamaican childhood stories / Earl McKenzie
School ed.

    p. : ill. ; cm
ISBN 978—976-8245-65-6 (pbk)

1 Children stories, Jamaican   2. Children's literature, Jamaican
3. Jamaican fiction
I.   Title

813   dc 23

Dedication

To Trudy, and with thanks to Carol Bender,
Kim Robinson Walcott and Sonia O. Jones,
and in memory of Roseanne Hoefel,
Joyce Patterson, Adlyn White
and E.A. Gregory.

Contents

Bobbing Jones

D udley was tall, gap-toothed and jovial. He seemed to be in his late twenties and it was said that he already had eighteen children scattered in several districts. He spent most of his time on the road, and had developed a reputation for his agility in hopping trucks and buses; none was too fast for him to get on or off. He liked making dramatic get-offs at places like squares where he had an audience, but his favourite get-off was to pretend to fall flat on his bottom in the middle of the road. He lived with an aunt and, although he had no visible occupation, never seemed to be without money. There were times when he disappeared from the district for long periods and no one knew where he went, but there would be occasional rumours of people seeing him at unexpected places down the country.

Ossie liked meeting him on the road, for each time they met Dudley had something new and interesting to tell or show. He was full of riddles, tricks and games, and he often showed Ossie well-made toys which he had made himself, presumably for his children.

Once Ossie met him on his way home from school and he asked Ossie a riddle which he could not guess. Dudley stood in the road and grinned and said:

"Riddle me dis and riddle me dat, guess me dis riddle and perhaps not. Hell at the top and hell at the bottom and halleluiah in the middle."

Ossie proposed a few answers, but Dudley rejected them all.

"I give up," said Ossie.

"Potato pudding!" laughed Dudley. "You bake it by putting fire at the top and fire at the bottom. And the sweet pudding is in the middle."

On another occasion Ossie met him while he was on his way to the bushes to pick breadfruits for his mother.

"I can make a needle float in a glass of water," said Dudley.

"I don't believe it," said Ossie.

"Well, you try it. Float a piece of paper on top of the water and rest the needle on the paper. The paper will absorb the water and then sink. But the needle will be left floating."

Ossie never got around to trying it, but it sounded reasonable enough.

One day Dudley showed Ossie a Bobbing Jones. It was made from wood and was H-shaped with the bottom section shorter than the top. There was a bar of string inserted in a special way at the top, and a wooden figure of a man hung from the bar. The figure was flat and had loose joints at the hips and shoulders. When Dudley pressed the bottom of the toy the figure performed acrobatic feats; when he released the pressure it hung motionless. Ossie was intrigued with the toy and offered to swap it for three of the beefy mangoes he had in the basket on his head. Dudley was pleased with the exchange and they made the swap. Then Dudley showed Ossie a few acrobatic feats of his own. He held his palms in front of him, and without letting go, carried his arms over his head and under his feet; his arms went round and round. Then he bent backwards and did a crab-walk with his hands and feet. He got up, winked at Ossie, and went on his way down the road.

One summer afternoon, at about three o' clock, the rain swept across the north-eastern hills and valleys- and poured down heavily on the village. Ossie could hear the rain hitting their zinc roof. He liked to hear the sound of the rain for it gave the house a cozy feeling. He cleared the centre table, took out his drawing-book and began to draw. The book had been given to him by Miss Princess, the postmistress; his mother had shown her some of his drawings, and she had copied them with tracing paper, and embroidered them onto her curtains and pillow-cases. Ossie was pleased to see his drawings being appreciated in this way, and now when he drew he kept Miss Princess in mind; he preferred to draw motor vehicles, buildings and boxers, but he also drew plants and animals since she liked these. He looked up from his drawing and glanced at his father who was dozing in the rocking chair. His mother was sewing in her bedroom; she sewed with her machine on the bed while she sat on a bench. Sometimes she earned money by making clothes for people in the district. During the lull between showers Ossie could hear the sound of her sewing machine.

Someone knocked urgently on the front door.

"Hoy! Anybody here?"

The voice sounded familiar. Ossie got up and opened the door.

Maas Man-Man, a distant relative of theirs, was standing on the verandah. Ossie turned and called his father. "Papa! Maas Man-Man come to you." His father got up and came out onto the verandah.

"Come help us catch the yam t'ief," said Maas Man-Man.

"Which t'ief? Where?"

"Maas Percy caught Dudley in his field t'iefing his afu yam. He used the rain as a cover, but Maas Percy and some other men were sheltering in Maas Percy's hut and saw him."

"It can't be Dudley!" cried Ossie.

They ignored him.

"The news spread fast," said Maas Man-Man. "They are now chasing him up the river bed. We need some men to block him from the other end."

"I am coming," said Ossie's father. He went into the bedroom and came out quickly wearing his hard boots and carrying a crocus bag for covering. "He made his first bad move," he said as he put on the bag, "t'iefing in his own district."

"I am coming," said Ossie.

"No you are not!" shouted his mother from her bedroom. "You are staying right here!"

Ossie watched as his father and Maas Man-Man disappeared in the rain. He watched the rain pelting the garden, the grapefruit tree and the patch of sugar cane. "Why did Dudley steal?" he wondered aloud, as if the rain had the answer. Now they were hunting him like an animal in the bushes. Ossie returned to the sitting-room but he could no longer draw. He leaned back in the chair, closed his eyes and listened to the humming of his mother's machine.

When the rain stopped, his mother sent him to the shop to buy a red herring to accompany the roast breadfruit she planned for breakfast the following morning. At the shop Ossie found a crowd of men, women and children. They were talking about the theft. Ossie gathered from the conversation that they were waiting for Dudley's captors to arrive with him. Ossie joined the crowd and waited. He listened to what the people were saying.

"We older folk do all the planting," said Maas Harry who had a graying beard. "The younger people don't want to work. All they want to do is t'ief."

"They should kill every t'ief," said Desmond with his eyes flaring.

He was a day-labourer who sometimes worked for Ossie's father.

"Beat them to death is what I say. That is what they are doing elsewhere, and I agree with them."

"And what about his children?" asked a pretty young woman in a blue dress.

"He isn't minding them anyway," replied Desmond. "He only gives them playthings."

"I didn't know he was a big-time t'ief," said Miss Enid the shopkeeper. She was a motherly woman with a mole on her right cheek. "He is so charming when he speaks to me."

"That is because you don't keep your ears close to the ground," said a fat woman who Ossie had not seen before.

They heard the shouts and curses before the captors arrived with their captive in front of the shop. Dudley was shirtless and his trousers were muddy and torn in many places. His back was covered with weals and he was bleeding from the mouth. His hands were handcuffed behind his back, and Mr. Richards, the district constable, led him by the waist. Maas Percy walked behind him. They were surrounded by other men. A smaller group of men followed and Ossie noticed that his father and Maas Man-Man were in this group. Mr. Richards, a muscular man with a deep voice, stopped and talked to the people at the shop.

"We caught him between two rocks near the river head. They beat him and somebody pushed a knife through his cheek. I had a hard time preventing the men from killing him. Let justice be done. Let the court decide his punishment."

Dudley did not turn to look at the people at the shop. He kept his eyes fixed to the ground. Ossie was glad he did not look up; he knew the laughing Dudley and now he did not want to see the pain in his eyes. When Mr. Richards had finished speaking he turned to his helpers and they continued on their way. Ossie noticed that Dudley was barefooted and was having difficulty walking on the stony road. Perhaps he had lost his shoes while they were chasing him.

When Ossie returned home his mother was still at her sewing, and she was singing choruses as she sewed. She told him to put the herring on the table; she would put it away later. Ossie felt haunted in the house; he did not know what to do with himself. Then he remembered the Bobbing Jones and went into his room to get it. He took it to the sitting-room, sat down and began playing with it. When he pressed the bottom he never knew which posture the figure would assume, just as he could never have foreseen the change in Dudley.

A Voting Man

O
ssie heard his father laughing on the verandah. He left the sitting-room and went out to see what was happening. There was a pig in the yard with a 'Vote PLP' placard hanging around its neck. The pig belonged to Maas Enos, their bearded neighbor, who was a People's Labour Party (PLP) supporter. Maas Enos knew that his pig came to their yard after breakfast each morning to see what it could get, so he had decided to use the animal to promote his political preference.

A few mornings later, Maas Delroy, a slim man with a receding hairline, and a Jamaica National Party (JNP) supporter, had breakfast with them. He had come to help Ossie's father castrate a pig, and afterwards they ate and discussed politics. Ossie heard him trying to convince his father that he should vote for the JNP.

"The JNP going to win the election," said Maas Delroy. "All the signs pointing that way."

"Which signs?" asked Ossie's father.

"I cut off the tops of two banana suckers and named one JNP and the other PLP. The JNP grew before the PLP. A sure sign that. And another thing, I filled two quart bottles of water and I named one JNP and the other PLP. I started emptying both at the same time. The JNP finished before the PLP. I have been predicting elections for years, and these signs have never failed me yet."

Ossie's father chuckled.

"I never vote for a party," he said. "I vote for the person I think is the better candidate."

"But you should back the winning team, man," said Maas Delroy. "That way you vote PIP, Party In Power, and you don't get left out."

Ossie did not know much about politics. When his teacher asked the class to name ministers of government, he had named the minister of their church. For the first time he realized that there were other kinds of ministers. But Ossie knew that an election was coming, that cars with loudspeakers would pass through the district announcing meetings, and that some of these meetings would be held in the square. There would be an election day and the grown-ups would vote. In the night they would gather around radios to listen to the results. There would be bets on who would win. After the results were known some people would be happy and others would be dejected.

One day Ossie saw his first politician at close range. He had delivered a parcel of clothes to one of his mother's customers and he was on his way home. He saw a big red car and a bus trying to pass each other on the narrow road. The bus passed safely and drove on, but the car slipped off the road and half of it sank into a ditch along the roadside. A chocolate-complexioned man with curly hair got out of the car; he was wearing a white shirt and striped pants. He studied Ossie carefully as Ossie approached him.

"Young fellow," he said, "please go and get help. Get some men to help me. Tell them Ronald Turner needs help."

Ossie knew the name; the man was the PLP candidate for the constituency. He went to Miss Enid's shop and found a few men there. He told them what happened.

"So Ronald Turner is in the ditch," said Maas Delroy. "Serves him right. I hear he has been giving guns to the youths."

"Lie!" said Maas Enos. "You cannot prove your allegation. I would not support him if he was doing that."

"That is what I heard," said Maas Delroy, "and where there is smoke there is fire."

"Come let us go and help him," said Ossie's father.

"Sure," said Maas Delroy. "I will help him. But this is not the only ditch he is in."

Word spread around the district and soon a team of men was helping to pull Mr. Turner's car out of the ditch. They used a rope and, after a lot of effort, they managed to get the car back on the road. It was the biggest and most beautiful car Ossie had ever seen and he said so. Mr. Turner told them he brought it from America when he decided to return home to serve his country.

"You should thank God you got back on the road," said Maas Delroy.

"God?" said Mr. Turner. "Had I asked God to get this car out of the ditch it would still be there. It is you I should thank, and I thank you very much."

"Are you denying God the praise?" asked Maas Delroy.

"I am giving thanks where it is due," said Mr. Turner.

"Are you an atheist?" asked Ossie's father.

"Yes, but that is a negative term. I use what is a more positive one. I am a secular humanist."

"What does that mean?" asked Maas Delroy.

"I won't go into it. But I believe man is on his own in the universe, and it is up to us to make this world a better place. You could call it self-reliance."

"The fool says in his heart there is no God," said Ossie's father.

"The man who said that was a believer," said Mr. Turner. "What else could you expect from him?"

"Is that the view of your party?" asked Maas Delroy.

"No," said Mr. Turner. "Most of the people in my party are believers. But I am not one of them. I have travelled a lot and seen too much evil to believe what they believe. Anyway, I believe in self-help. If I'm elected, I will help you to help yourselves. I plan to introduce self-help projects in agriculture, housing and cottage industries. We are going to build this constituency with our own creativity and labour. We are going to use your ideas. But we can talk about that later. Right now I want to show my appreciation. Let me buy all of you a drink. I will park the car and then we can go to the shop."

Some of the men went with him to the shop. The others, perhaps outraged by his lack of religion or the rumour about guns, stayed away. Ossie noticed that his father was among those who stayed away.

One day Mr. James Townsend, the JNP candidate, and the sitting member of parliament for the constituency, came to Ossie's home to ask for his father's vote. Ossie and his father were sitting on the verandah when Mr. Townsend and his entourage entered the yard. He was a fat and fair-complexioned man with straight hair and was the owner of a trucking company. Ossie had seen him at their church from time to time. His father got up and shook hands with Mr. Townsend; then he called his wife from the kitchen and introduced her. Mr. Townsend began his speech:

"Our party stands for godliness and freedom. We have also built the most roads in the entire history of the constituency. And we have big plans. We are going to build a tank at the East River, and we are going to put in a pump powerful enough to pump water up here. We are going to build a cocoa factory. We plan to bring electricity and improve the transportation system. I am asking you for your vote. Vote JNP and vote for progress."

"He is the hardest-working MP we have ever had," said a member of his entourage.

After some light conversation, Mr. Townsend and his followers moved on to another home.

One morning, after breakfast, Maas Delroy brought the news. They were giving out road work and men were being signed up. Ossie's father pulled his hoe and shovel from under the house and set off. He came home about half-an-hour later and returned his tools to their place under the floor. His wife asked him what had happened, but he refused to talk. He said he was going to his field in the valley to prepare the land for the corn and gungo peas he would soon plant.

Later, at the shop, Ossie heard what had happened to his father. He heard it from Maas Enos who was telling some other men at the shop. His father had arrived at the work site and found Chesty, who was signing up the men. Chesty was a muscular young man who always wore T-shirts and dark glasses. He had a clipboard and he was writing down the names of the men who were being employed. When it was Ossie's father's turn Chesty said, "Which party do you belong to?"

Ossie's father explained that he voted for the candidate and not the party.

"So you are a ping-pong ball," said Chesty. "You bounce from one party to the next."

"I exercise my judgement."

"Well, you not getting any work here. We want people who support the cause. Only supporters of Townsend getting work."

"Is that his wish?"

"Townsend is boss! Townsend rules!"

Ossie's father turned around and returned to his home.

"Victimization!" said Maas Enos, thumping his fist on the counter.

"Your party does it too," said Maas Delroy.

"I don't deny that," said Maas Enos.

"And it is wrong whoever does it," said Maas Delroy.

The following day would be Good Friday. Ossie's home was full of the aroma of Easter buns. Ossie thought of the things which would occupy his attention on Good Friday. At sunrise he would watch the sun to see if it danced as the grown-ups said it did on that day. He would breakfast on bun and cheese and hot chocolate. They would go to church. He would refuse to chop the oil-nut tree to see if it would groan and bleed as the grown-ups said it did on Good Friday. But he would go from yard to yard to look at the glasses of water and egg-white that people would put in the sun to predict the future; most of them usually saw ships, wedding cakes and coffins; but now, perhaps, some would see a hoe, the symbol of the PLP, or a fist, the symbol of the JNP.

But before he did any of those things, he would go to the field with his father to plant corn and gungo peas. It was widely believed that if these crops were planted on Good Friday they would be more fruitful.

Early on Good Friday morning, while the birds were singing in the trees, Ossie and his father set off for the field. His father went before him down the hillside path; he carried his hoe slung over his shoulder. Ossie followed with a cloth bag made by his mother; the bag contained the corn and gungo peas mixed together. His father would dig the holes and Ossie would throw three grains of corn and three grains of gungo peas into each hole. They would have finished planting by sunrise.

"Do you plan to vote, Papa?" asked Ossie.

"Yes. I have never refused to exercise my right to vote. It is a hard-won and very important right. Think of the many people in the world who aren't allowed to vote."

"But who are you going to vote for?"

"The better man."

"Who is that?"

"I won't tell you. That is my secret. I don't have to tell that to anybody."

Ossie glanced at his father's hoe. He noticed that the cutting edge was badly worn, and that he would soon need a new one. But there was still some work left in it. Ossie hoped the corn would grow into big, healthy stalks, and that the gungo peas would flourish.

The Bamboo Fife

The headmaster said that all pupils should take their handi-crafts to school, and that he would show the best ones to the Inspector on Inspection Day. A boy named Leroy Lindsay brought a bamboo fife and, before handing it in, he showed it around. He played it in the school-yard at recess time and a crowd of children gathered around him to listen to his music. They applauded him after each piece he played. He was the star of the recess period and, after playing for the crowd, he strutted around the school-yard with the fife stuck under his belt.

Ossie had never seen a fife before and he was fascinated. He followed Leroy around waiting for a chance to talk to him about the fife. Leroy stood on the stonewall where he could watch the girls playing hop-scotch, and where they could see him with his fife. Ossie sat on the wall near to him.

"Leroy," said Ossie, "where you got that fife?"

"I made it myself, man," said Leroy.

"Really? How?"

"Easy," said Leroy, pulling the fife from his belt so he could demonstrate how easy it was to make one. "First you must choose the right kind of bamboo; it must be ripe, dry, long and straight. You cut off the joints at both ends. Then you measure the space for the holes. You put one hole up here to blow into, and six down here to change the sound. You can use the thing carpenters use to bore holes, or you can use the head of a red-hot nail. Then you stop up the top end with an English cork and you ready to play. Easy!"

That evening Ossie took his father's machete and headed for the nearest bamboo grove. Now that he was looking for one, it seemed as if there were dozens of potential fifes in the grove. He searched carefully until he found a bamboo that seemed just right; it was bone dry, light yellow in colour, and it had long, even segments.

After some deliberation he made a mental note of the segment he would use, and then he set off for home.

He spent the following week preparing to make the fife. He got an English cork from the village shopkeeper. His grandfather lent him a four-inch nail and he used a bit of hardwood to make a handle for it. He used his father's knife – it was the sharpest in the house – to remove the chosen segment from the rest of the bamboo pole.

Then, on Saturday evening, while he was cooking dinner for their pig, he heated the nail in the wood-fire and bored the holes. The nail's head went through the bamboo easily, and a gush of smoke was sent up each time he bored a hole. The burnt holes gave the fife a pleasant aroma. After he had bored the holes, he corked the end near the single hole and the fife was now ready to be played.

He covered the six holes with three fingers of his left hand, and the corresponding three fingers of his right hand. Then, with his fingers trembling with excitement, he raised the single hole to his lips and blew. After a few attempts the sound came easily. Then he found that he was able to change the sound by covering and uncovering the six holes.

Ossie loved the sound of his fife. He sat on the mortar in the kitchen and practiced. Before long he knew the sound which was produced by the movement of each finger, and he began putting notes together to form tunes he knew. By nightfall he was able to play 'Abide With Me', a hymn he had learnt at church. He was working on 'Santa Lucia', a song he was taught at school, when his mother returned from the shop.

"Boy, mind you call up snakes out of the bush!" she called to him from the back door of the house. "Is what that you playing?"

"A fife, ma'am."

"Where you got it?"

"I made it myself, ma'am."

"Tan! You turn musician on me. You feed the pig yet?"

'No, 'm.'

"What! You go and feed that pig this minute! And I don't want to hear any more noise in the place."

Ossie fed the pig. The he returned to the mortar in the kitchen and played 'Abide With Me', a few more times. His mother came to the back door again.

"But you not too bad, boy," she said. "You really know how to play the thing. But didn't I tell you to stop the noise? I am tired and I am not too far from mi bed."

That night Ossie slept with his fife on the table beside his pillow. He dreamt that he was playing it in front of a large audience. Each piece he played met with enthusiastic applause. The loudest applause came after he played a tune which was his own composition. Notes of music floated through his dreams all night. Next morning he was awakened by the singing of birds.

The following week, nearly every boy in the school carried a fife stuck under his belt. Recess time was a cacophony of fifes but since only a few of the boys knew how to play, the fashion soon waned. Ossie continued playing his fife and he gradually added new tunes to his repertoire. But his own enthusiasm eventually cooled, and he began leaving his fife in odd places around the house, forgetting where it was. There were days, and even weeks, when he did not play it at all.

One evening at dusk, while he was studying in his room, he heard the music of a fife which seemed to come from the verandah of their house. Though only a few notes, they were expertly delivered, and better than anything he had ever heard from Leroy Lindsay. It was music which he dimly remembered but could not identify. He went out to the verandah to see who was playing the fife, but there was no one there. His fife was lying on the chair where he had left it.

A week or so later, Ossie heard the mysterious fife player again. He was on his way home from school and, as he approached the house, he heard the music seemingly coming from the kitchen. But when he went to the kitchen there was no one there. The fife was lying on the table where he had left it.

Ossie felt like talking to his parents about the mysterious fife player, but thought that they would tell him it was a duppy and laugh at him. Besides, his parents frequently accused him of imagining things, and they were likely to regard this as just another instance of his over-active imagination. He decided to try and solve the mystery on his own.

The phantom fife player, he noticed, played the fife when he left it lying around. The solution, he decided, was to be more careful about where he left the fife. He put it in the drawer by his bedside and waited to see what would happen.

For a few weeks nothing did happen. Then one night while he was returning home from the shop he heard the fife music which seemed to come from the house. As he drew closer he discovered that the music was in fact coming from the verandah. There was a light in the sitting-room, but the verandah was in darkness.

Ossie walked stealthily and kept to the bank so that he could not be easily seen. He crept to the corner of the house and waited. The music was now loud and clear. How, he wondered, could a duppy play so well?

With his heart thumping, and in one quick movement, he ran across to the entrance and then up the verandah steps. In the glow of the light from the windows of the drawing-room he immediately made out the figure of his father. He was sitting on a chair and playing the fife. Ossie sat on the other chair and listened. His father finished the piece he was playing and started another. It was the best fife music Ossie had ever heard and made Leroy Lindsay look like a fumbling beginner. His father's music described a world which was only vaguely familiar to Ossie, but which his father obviously knew very well.

"I didn't know you can play fife, Papa," said Ossie when his father stopped playing.

His father chuckled.

"I used to play fife in a band when I was a young man. Parson Roper from the Baptist Church started that band, and the conductor was Captain Robinson, a retired band leader from the army. That man knew music! He could play every instrument in the band. When he died the band broke up."

"Why you didn't keep on playing?"

Ossie's father was silent for a long time, and his silence was heavy with difficult explanations.

"When it comes to music," he said, finally breaking his silence, "I know sound and I know time. I wanted to become a musician, but life pushed me in a different direction. When I left high school my father gave me a hoe and a machete and told me I was on my own. I played the fife for fun for a while, but I didn't keep it up."

"That was a pity, Papa."

"I didn't even know that I can still play. I heard you with your fife, and I tried it out a few times when I saw it lying around. Tonight I was really in the mood to play and I asked your mother to help me find it."

"What is that kind of music that you play?"

"Old-time mento. That was the music in my day."

"Play some more."

Ossie's father played a few more tunes, then he handed the fife to Ossie. "Let me hear you now," he said.

Ossie played 'My Bonnie Lies Over the Ocean', his latest accomplishment.

"Not bad, son," his father said, "not bad at all. Maybe you will carry on where I left off."

"Ossie, bring the milk!" he heard his mother calling from the dining room. "Oonuh break up the concert and come for supper."

Ossie crossed the sitting-room and went into the dining-room.

"Heaven help me," he heard his mother say. "Now it is two of them I have in the house!"

Cricket Season

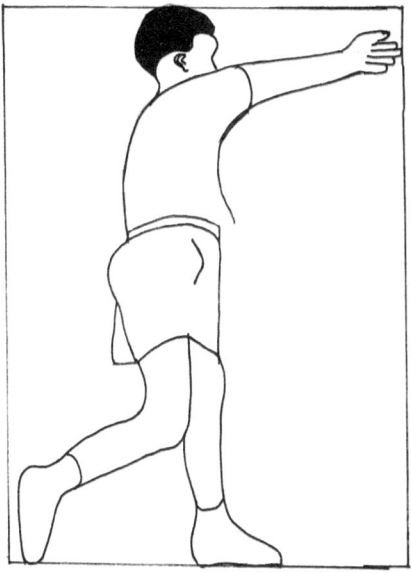

Uncle Basil, the soldier, gave Ossie money as a gift the day before he returned to England. Ossie met him on the parochial road. He came up the slope wearing his felt hat, white shirt and brown tweed trousers, and he stopped to talk with Ossie. He had bright, intelligent eyes which looked at Ossie kindly, but Ossie also noticed a touch of sadness in them; he retired home to a hero's welcome after each promotion, but they said he cried each time he had to leave. Ossie loved his stories and photographs of the places he had visited. He remembered Ossie and stopped and talked with him each time they met.

"Ossie, you are walking like a big shot," said Uncle Basil, grinning. "Seems you own the place, man."

Ossie laughed.

"What games do you play?" asked Uncle Basil. Each time they met they talked about a different topic. The last time they had talked about school.

"I like cricket," said Ossie.

"Are you a batsman or a bowler?"

"A bowler. A spin bowler."

"A spin bowler, eh. Maybe you will be another Alfred Valentine. We have had lots of talented cricketers in these parts, but so far no one has made it to the national team. But maybe you will."

Uncle Basil reached into his pocket, took out a coin and gave it to Ossie.

"Thank you, Uncle Basil," said Ossie. He was thrilled. Nobody had ever given him so much money before.

"I am leaving tomorrow," said Uncle Basil. "Don't know when I'll be back. You may be a big boy then." He began walking up the road.

"Bye, Uncle Basil."

"And when you bowl remember this – keep your eyes on the stumps."

When Ossie got home he saw his father chopping wood in the yard in front of the kitchen. He told him about the money that Uncle Basil had given him. His father stopped chopping the wood and looked at him.

"You should save it," said his father. "I will show you how. Just a minute."

His father went into the house and returned with his saw.

"Follow me," he said, as he led the way into the kitchen. He chose a bamboo joint on one of the kitchen posts – choosing one which was in Ossie's reach – and, using his saw, he cut a slit near the top of the joint.

"This is your savings box," he said. "Put in the money."

Ossie slipped the coin into the opening and heard it drop to the bottom of the joint.

"When you have enough saved you cut the bottom of the joint and take out your money. That was how I used to save money when I was a boy. Now save your money and get rich."

His father returned to the yard to continue chopping wood. Ossie decided to save up to buy a cricket book. He found ways of increasing his earnings, and his savings grew in the bamboo joint. He collected cocoa beans that fell from the pods eaten by rats, dried them in the sun, and sold them to Miss Enid the shop-keeper. When he saw fit soursops on trees he picked them and asked the higglers to sell them in Kingston. He made yo-yos and gigs and sold them to boys at school. He weeded his aunts' gardens and got paid for his labour.

Then the cricket season came. The West Indies team was playing against England at Sabina Park, and the excitement spread even to the remote villages in the hills. Men gathered at the shops to listen to the commentary on the radio. Each day at the school the headmaster left his desk to play with the boys in the school yard. He was a big man who hit powerful fours and sixes, and small boys spent hours searching for the balls that landed in the bushes. A match was planned between a team from Ossie's village and one from another village some miles away. It would be played in the churchyard on a Sunday afternoon.

Small boys did not get to play with the headmaster; neither were they selected for the matches between villages. But they enjoyed the game nevertheless. They made bats from coconut fronds and, using stones as stumps, played the game in the road. The big boys who played well were their heroes; and they argued about their favourites among the test cricketers whom they heard described on the radio.

Ossie began making a cricket ball. First he carved a spheroid from a bamboo root. Then he wrapped it tightly in a piece of cloth. After this he knitted a thick covering over it; the covering was made from string and he used a nail to do the knitting. The knitted patterns made the ball very attractive. The covering of string would give the ball its bounce.

The day of the cricket match arrived.

In the morning, Ossie and his parents went to church. Ossie's father did not go to church often; on Sundays he liked to sleep late and then relax at home dressed in pants and vest; but his wife sometimes persuaded him to go. On this occasion she said that the church would be welcoming a new minister, and a large turnout would make a good impression. So he put on his navy-blue suit and accompanied them to church.

When they returned home they changed into their Sunday-evening clothes. Ossie sat in the sitting-room and skimmed through a religious picture-book while he waited for dinner to be served. His mother passed through the sitting-room on her way to the kitchen. A few moments later he heard her cry out in the kitchen. "T'ief! T'ief!" she cried. Ossie rushed to the kitchen.

"The dinner is gone!" his mother exclaimed. "The pot with the curried chicken and the pot with the rice. Both gone!"

Ossie turned to look inside the bamboo joint which contained his money. The thief had chopped an opening at the bottom of the joint. Ossie stuck a finger in and found it empty.

"My money gone!" he wailed. "All the money I saved!"

His father came into the kitchen and they told him what had happened.

"They watched us," he said. "They knew I wasn't here. And it is somebody who has been here before, somebody who had the time to notice Ossie's savings box."

Ossie thought of the faceless persons who had caused this distress. They were people who struck when you were not there to defend yourself. Perhaps they were people he knew, who had other faces – ones of evil that he had never seen.

"Perhaps they are hungrier than we are," said his mother charitably.

"The food is bad enough," said his father, "but to steal from a child!"

"Uncle Basil would be very sorry to hear they stole the money he gave me," said Ossie.

"But he would want you to continue saving," said his mother.

They had sardines, bread and tomatoes for their dinner.

After eating, Ossie got his ball and set off for the churchyard to watch the match. If the match ended early he would probably be able to play with his friends. He was hoping that the big boys would not capture the pitch after the game. The team from Ossie's village won the match after a close and exciting contest. The hero of the team was Vincent, a slim sixteen-year old with straight hair. Vincent was the son of a prosperous truck operator. It was well-known that Vincent did poorly at school. But, put a bat in his hand and he was transformed: he became expressive, confident and masterful. He said things with his bat that he could not put into words. Today he gave one of his best performances and led his team to victory.

After the match, men and boys followed Vincent and other members of the team to the stonewall. Ossie was so thrilled by Vincent's performance that he forgot about playing and followed Vincent and his admirers. They sat on the wall and discussed the match. In the heat of the discussion, some of Vincent's admirers, on remembering a feature of his performance, went up to him and shook his hand. Ossie sat on the base of the wall and listened while fiddling with his cricket ball.

Vincent was so elated with his performance he wanted to continue playing. He took the stumps from Reggie, the manager of the team, and set them up in the road. Then he took a ten-dollar bill from his wallet and held it up in the air.

"Any man who bowl me get this money," he said.

"Give me the money to hold," said Reggie, a fat young man in a colourful shirt and blue pants.

25

Vincent gave Reggie the money.

Boys rushed forward to take their turns bowling to Vincent. But he was too good for them. He played virtually every stroke in the book. He talked to the bowlers while he batted, and he hit each ball with scorn and contempt.

"Nobody can bowl him," said Reggie. "He is seeing that ball as big as a breadfruit."

But the bowlers persisted. It would soon be dark. They wanted to get him before bad light stopped play. Ossie went out to bowl. There was loud laughter from some of the men and boys. But a few of them cheered him on. Vincent grinned when he saw Ossie.

"Don't laugh!" shouted Phonso. "Ossie is a good bowler." Ossie faced Vincent. He remembered Uncle Basil's words: *Keep your eyes on the stumps.* He studied Vincent for a few moments thinking about some of his characteristic movements. Then he ran up and, aiming at the stumps, bowled. Vincent shouted "No!" as he played the ball back to Ossie. Ossie bowled again, getting the ball to spin more this time and it beat Vincent and hit the middle stump.

"Clean bowled!" the shout went up from the wall.

"Lucky ball nothing," said Reggie. "He was bowled fair and square."

"He said any 'man' who could bowl him," said another boy, "he didn't say any 'boy'."

Reggie laughed. "Come take your money, Ossie," he said.

Grinning happily, Ossie took the money and pocketed it.

"Good ball, Ossie!" shouted Vincent as he went by.

The session was now over and the men and boys left for their homes.

Ossie's parents were having supper when he rushed into the house; he joined them and shared the news of his good fortune. His father laughed. "You made a fast comeback. You are earning money from cricket and you are not a test player yet."

"Isn't that more than you lost today?" asked his mother.

"Yes."

"Imagine that, eh?"

"Are you still going to save it?" asked his father.

"Yes. I may never know who stole my money. Let them take it. But I am not putting this in a bamboo joint."

"Bamboo joints are not as safe as when I was a boy," said his father.

"I heard Teacher talking about a post office bank," said Ossie. "I am going to find out more about it."

"It is now you are going to want to buy that cricket book," said his mother.

Ossie grinned. "I am going to study bowling. It has been good to me."

Brother Paul

"**W**ake up, Ossie." His mother's voice sounded very far away. Then he felt her shaking his left shoulder. "Wake up, Ossie. Get up and put on your school clothes."

Ossie sat up and looked around the room. It was still dark. "School clothes, Mama? And it is still before-day."

"You not going to school today. You going to see Brother Paul, the healer."

"Brother Paul!"

"Shut up. Not a word out of you. Not a word of this to anybody. You must learn to keep your mouth shut."

Ossie could not believe he was hearing correctly. He was going to see Brother Paul! His staunchly Anglican mother was sending him to see a healer!

"I am making some tea for you," his mother said as she walked towards the door. "Come around to the kitchen when you finish getting ready."

Ossie got dressed and went outside. He took a calabash of water from the barrel beside the house, walked over to the hibiscus hedge and washed his mouth and face. He returned to the house and dried himself and combed his hair. Then he went outside to the kitchen.

His mother handed him a mug of fever-grass tea, and a plate with a warmed-up, leftover dumpling and two slices of buttered hard-dough bread. Ossie sat on the mortar and sipped the hot drink. But he had no desire for the dumpling and the bread. His mother put a few pieces of wood in the fire. "Your Uncle Tony and Uncle Freddie going to see him too," she said. "They will be waiting for you at the church gate." She started blowing the fire to keep the flames alive. The smoke came up into her face and she turned away and coughed. "I hope this will work," she said when she was finished coughing. "I don't know what kind of headache you have that won't go away. Doctor after doctor after doctor. And none of them can find the reason for it. Eat fast. Don't let them have to wait for you."

After he had eaten all he could, Ossie put the rest on the dresser. "Is that all you can eat?" asked his mother. "Eat more. You going have to walk far, you know. Eat some more."

"I can't eat anymore, ma'am."

"Take this," she said, handing him some money.

Ossie thanked her and put the money in his pocket.

"Gone Mama," he said as he walked out of the kitchen.

"Ok, mi love," she said. "Walk good."

Ossie started walking towards the main road. A few fowls were coming up out of the bushes from their roosts. It would soon be daylight.

At the church gate he found his uncles waiting. They started walking down the road as soon as they saw him. He had to walk quickly to keep up with them. As they walked they made occasional comments to each other about their crops, families, and the political situation in the country. But they did not speak to him at all.

Brother Paul had his Mission House at the top of the neighbouring ridge in the east. As they followed the main road they could hear the well-known rhythm of his drum: three strong beats followed by a pause. They knew that the drumming would go on until the sun was above the top of the mountain.

It was about an hour's walk to the Mission House. They had to go down into the valley, cross the Piaba River, and then climb the steep side of the ridge up to the healer's district. As he walked behind his uncles Ossie thought about Brother Paul. He imagined a biblical man with a long beard, long flowing robe, and wild visionary eyes. He was probably also very strong since it was well-known that he sometimes beat the sinners who went to see him. He could read the secrets of the heart, people said, and before he reached for his rod of chastisement, he often recited, in the most minute details, the misdeeds of strangers he was seeing for the first time.

Ossie tried recalling his own misdeeds, and he wondered if the healer would see them. He repented of all his wrong-doings, remembered and unremembered. He hoped there would be no evil in him for the holy man to see.

It seemed cool and early in the shadow of the valley, but when they got to the top of the ridge they found that the sun was already high in the sky. They started walking along the main road towards the Mission House and they could hear the sound of lusty singing in the distance.

A loaded taxi passed them going in the same direction. "Same place they going," said Uncle Tony. "People come here from all over the island. Sometimes they come by the truck-load." Then they met a group of well-dressed people going in the opposite direction.

"The morning service over," observed Uncle Freddie.

"They go on all day," said Uncle Tony. They turned a corner and found themselves in full view of the Mission House. Ossie felt his heart pounding wildly at the sight of the beautiful white church on the hillside above the main road. He had not expected anything so striking; he had thought that healers had their meetings only in little bamboo churches. The Mission House was surrounded by a wide yard with a low and neatly pruned hibiscus hedge. Throngs of people where moving in and out of the building, standing around in the yard and, as in the Bible story, were ascending and descending the long flight of steps which linked the Mission House to the main road. Most of the people wore thick turbans and long, flowing robes of white, purple and red. From inside the Mission House came the frenzied sounds of singing, drums and tambourines. They climbed the steps to the door of the Mission House.

"Have you come to see the Shepherd?" asked a tall woman in purple at the door.

"Yes," said Uncle Tony.

The woman pointed to a pair of long benches along the right wall. The front bench was already full of patients.

"Sit down and wait your turn," said the woman. They put Ossie in front and joined the line.

The singers and musicians occupied a central rectangle, and the benches were arranged around them. Ossie looked around at this different kind of church. Huge pictures of religious subjects decorated the walls. He was especially drawn to an immense mural above the altar; it showed a huge black angel – the first picture of a black angel that Ossie had ever seen – flying down from heaven to earth with an olive branch in his hand. The tiled floor was clean and polished. The air was full of a sweet and unfamiliar perfume. When the song ended, the leader of the singers raised her right hand for attention.

"And the question came up in heaven!" she shouted. "Who should go and save Adam's fallen race? And when no one volunteered, the Son Himself stepped forward and said, 'Father, here am I, send me'."

"Amen!" said the other singers and members of the congregation.

"And he came and shed His precious blood on Calvary!"

"Amen!"

"And He died to save us all!"

"Amen! Amen!"

"What a wonderful thing!"

"A wonderful thing!"

The drummers introduced the rhythm of the song.

"Sing," whispered Uncle Tony. "Sing before they pick on us." They joined in the singing of the song:

O what a wonderful thing
To be free from sin
And have Christ within,
To be a joint-heir
With Jesus my Lord
O what a wonderful, wonderful thing!

The healer had his office in a small room to the right of the assembly hall. To get to it, patients had to go outside and then enter through another door from there. The healer had a bell which he touched when he was ready for another patient. There was a peep-hole with a shutter built into the wall through which he could see the patient before the patient saw him.

With his heart pounding, Ossie waited for the sound of the bell. In a clear, authoritative tone the healer's signal finally came. Ossie stumbled down the steps to the door. He saw the flick of the shutter behind the peep-hole. For a moment he hesitated at the door.

"Come in!" said the healer's voice. Ossie pushed the door and entered the small room. The healer was seated behind his desk. He was a thin man of medium height, light-chocolate complexion, and thin, straight hair which was brushed back neatly. The most striking thing about him was his dark, brilliant, penetrating eyes. He wore a crisply-ironed khaki uniform which seemed military, but, because of the absence of pockets, appeared to be of his own design. There was also an open exercise-book with one of its pages covered with a continuous flow of zig-zag strokes. Ossie tried to read it but there were no words that he could recognize. Without saying anything to him, Brother Paul picked up his ball-point pen, closed his eyes, and started making a similar flow of zig-zag strokes on the other page.

"You have this bad feeling in your head," said Brother Paul, "and a foamy feeling in your stomach." He stopped talking, but with his eyes still closed, he kept marking while he waited for the words to come. Ossie looked around the room for the healer's rod, but there was nothing like it in sight. He looked at the portrait of Jesus on the wall behind the healer; the face seemed full of wisdom and compassion. Below the portrait were the words: 'The Great Physician'. Then Ossie looked at the framed quotations on the walls. They were all words that Jesus had used in healing people:

'And he put forth His hand and touched him saying, I will: be thou clean. And immediately the leprosy departed from him.'

'Young man, I say unto thee Arise.'

'Be of good comfort: thy faith has made thee whole: go in peace.'

"You going through a rough time," said the healer, in a soft and gentle voice. "But all you need is a little help, and you going to make it."

Ossie was amazed that the healer was taking him so seriously. Brother Paul had not shown the slightest surprise at the sight of a mere boy entering his office alone, and he was treating him as he would a grown-up. From the beads of perspiration which were forming on his forehead, it was clear that he was trying very hard to help him.

"You going have to watch your diet," the healer continued as he kept marking very rapidly. "No oils and fats. No pork at all. And drink plenty grapefruit juice."

The healer opened his eyes. He seemed very tired and drained. He took a slip of paper from a box, scribbled something on it, and handed it to Ossie.

"Give this to the man in the building outside. Let me see how you improving in two weeks." Ossie glanced at the paper, but he couldn't make anything out. It was written the same way the doctors wrote and so was hard to read.

"Should I go to school, sah?" asked Ossie.

"Sure," said the healer, with a slight suggestion of a smile in his eyes.

"Thank you, sah," said Ossie.

He opened the door and walked out into the warm sunshine. The building opposite the healer's room had a counter in front, and a big mulatto with a neatly trimmed moustache was serving bottles of medicine to the group of people gathered there. Ossie joined them and waited his turn. When he finally got to the counter, the man looked at his paper and told him he had to get his bath first. "The men's balm-yard is right behind here," he said. "Bring back the paper after you have had your bath."

Ossie took off his clothes in the designated area, and joined the group of nude men in the front section of the balm-yard. In the next section were several large wash-pans containing water and various wild herbs, some of which he recognized. As he was about to enter the balming section, the man who stood at the entrance poured a goblet of herb-scented water over him. Ossie yelled at the impact of the ice-cold water. The man chuckled and waved him on.

In the balming section Ossie faced the chief balmer. He was a fat, black man with wild ecstatic eyes. "There is a balm in Gilead!"

he yelled as he anointed Ossie's limbs, "and it shall wipe away all tears from your eyes, all tears from your eyes!" Ossie recognized the smell of the ointment as the same perfume he remembered from the assembly hall. After his balming, the balmer gave him a small vial of the ointment. "Use before you go to bed, and before you leave your house," he prescribed.

Ossie felt very cool and refreshed when he walked out into the sunshine again. He returned to the counter and the man gave him a bottle of dark medicine.

"One tablespoon after meals," he ordered. While he waited for his uncles, Ossie made a tour of the surroundings of the Mission House. There were many white pigeons flying around, and other birds in cages. There were also several well-kept flower gardens. Brother Paul had a reputation for being a lover of animals and flowers. Behind the Mission House compound was the house where the destitute women lived. Brother Paul provided free care for destitute women in exchange for their assistance in taking care of the Mission House.

Ossie stood at the eastern edge of the yard and looked across the mountain. He could see the river which ran down the mountain-side, visible from his home only when it rained heavily. As he watched the white streak of flowing water, he was reminded of the refreshing feeling of the balmer's herb-scented water flowing over his body. He felt cleansed and pure as the white river that shone in the light of the morning sun.

When they were finished, his uncles found him, and they all returned to the assembly hall and listened to the service for a while before leaving.

They stopped at a small shop and lunched on bun, cheese and sodas. They also bought a brown-paper bag for their bottles of medicine. Then they began the journey home. Ossie felt light and happy as he walked into the house. His mother sat on the bed beside him while he described the visit.

"I wasn't as afraid of him as I thought I was going to be," said Ossie. "I didn't think he would look like an ordinary man."

"He isn't an ordinary man, mi love," said his mother quietly. "Brother Paul is a very good man. He didn't go to college, like our rector, but he has a gift. He was born and raised in that same district and, when you see a prophet getting so much honour in his own country, it is a sign. By their fruits ye shall know them, saith the Lord. And Brother Paul is a blessing to his people."

Ossie began taking his medicine. It was pleasant-tasting and not like the medicine he got from the doctors. At night his mother anointed him with the ointment. There cannot be absolute certainty that Brother Paul was the cause of it, but by the middle of the following week his headache had disappeared.

Admission: Children Ten Cents

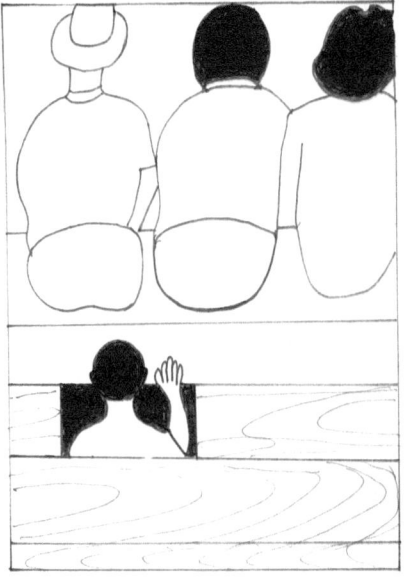

The headmaster's bell sounded and the children began leaving the classrooms row by row in an orderly fashion. "You going to show tonight, Ossie?" asked Phonso as soon as they were in the schoolyard.

"Show, which show?"

"Film show at St. Michael's Church tonight, man. Me must be there."

"How much to go in?"

"Ten cents for children and twenty cents for big people."

"I don't have any money."

"Ask your mother. All of us boys going. One-Son, Brightly, Washie. All of us. I wouldn't miss this for anything, boy. Is not often film-shows come to bush places like these."

"Is a cowboy show?"

"I don't know and I don't care. Show is show. All I know is that I will be there."

That evening after dinner Ossie mentioned the show to his mother. "Mama, I hear they having a sacred film-show at the church tonight." He thought that if he emphasized the word 'sacred' this might improve his chances.

"Is show sweet you, nuh?" she replied. "Before you go bring home the goats – you standing there before me talking about show! You don't see there isn't any water in the barrel? And you don't see I don't have any wood to boil tea in the morning? Show, show, show! You and nothing but show!"

With great speed Ossie brought home the goats, half-filled the barrel with water from the village tank, and collected a bundle of firewood which was nearly as large as those he usually collected on Saturdays. Then he waited patiently on the verandah. His mother kept humming as she went about her business around the house. Night fell and the stars came out. His mother continued to hum. He was at the point of tears when she called him into the room and gave him the ten cents for the show. He washed himself, pulled on his clothes, and shot off in the dark towards the church. At the church gate he found Phonso and the other boys sitting on the grass.

"The show-van don't come from Kingston yet," Phonso explained. "And nobody in the church yet either. But don't worry. They'll come. Everybody will come. Country people never start anything until everybody is ready. We ready too early, that's all." They were silent for a few moments, then Phonso spoke again, lowering his voice.

"Guess what. I know a way we can get in to see this show without paying."

"How?" asked Brightly.

"You know those round, swinging windows at the back? We can slip in through one of them."

"How you know that?" asked Brightly.

"Because I tried it myself earlier this evening. And left one open and fixed for tonight."

"Suppose they see us?" asked One-Son. "You know who the gateman going to be? Maas Rashie! And he is a man who don't joke, boy!"

"Cho!" scoffed Phonso. "He won't see us. We can go right now before the other people come."

"And what happen when they open the church and find us in there?" asked One-Son.

"They won't see us, quashie!" said Phonso with growing impatience. "We'll be up in the balcony."

"Whoy-oh!" One-Son exclaimed. "You must think Maas Rashie is fool-fool. If he is going to search anywhere, that is the one and only place he is going to search."

"But by the time he gets up there, we'll be under the floor, stupid! They are repairing the floor of the balcony. All you have to do is to slip underneath and nobody can see you."

"Anyway, it is wrong," said Washie, joining in. "It is wrong to t'ief your way into a church."

"I agree with that," said Philbert.

"Cho!" sneered Phonso. "Is coward oonuh coward. Oonuh fraidie-fraidie like puss. Awright, then. Brightly, Ossie and myself will go in right now. Then we will laugh at the idiots when we see you come in after paying your big ten cents. You know what I could do with ten cents? Come on, Brightly and Ossie. Let's go!"

Brightly got up.

"What happen, Ossie?" asked Phonso. "You not coming, man? You mean to tell me you are a coward like these yellow sissies, man? You fraidie-fraidie too? I am ashamed of you. You let me down, Ossie. You really let me down!" Ossie got up and joined them. Walking close together they passed through the columns at the gate. "If my old lady finds out about this I am in trouble," said Ossie. "She would kill me, man. Then she would tell my father and he would kill me worse."

"Cool man, cool," said Phonso. "Nobody going to find out. And you going to save ten cents. You think I would lead you into trouble, man?"

It was dark and lonely in the churchyard. Phonso led them towards the secret window at the back. They were almost there when they heard footsteps in the grass behind them. "Lean against the wall!" Phonso whispered and they quickly obeyed. Then they heard someone softly calling Phonso's same. It was One-Son. The others had decided to join them. Phonso led them to the window. He slipped through expertly, and one by one the others followed him.

Inside the church it was dark and spooky. Ghostly figures peered down at them from the stained-glass windows. The air was heavy with the smell of ratbats.

Following Phonso, they felt their way along the benches to the aisle; then they groped their way back and across to the foot of the stairway to the balcony. They went up quickly.

"See what I mean?" said Phonso triumphantly when they got to the top.

There was a strong smell of freshly planted wood and saw-dust. Phonso showed them a space in the floor all along the back of the balcony. They should slip under there, he said, if anyone came up. Ossie didn't like the idea. It would be hot and stuffy and it would be hard to breathe. And there would be ratbats. At Phonso's suggestion they sat along the back row close to the escape hatch. They sat in the dark and waited.

It seemed a long time before they heard the first voices downstairs as the door was opened. Someone brought in a gas lamp. The sounds of voices increased as more people entered. They heard the parson's strong, authoritative voice rising above those of others as he gave orders and greeted new arrivals. The van came and the men began putting up the screen and the projector. Outside, the electric plant started puttering.

Then suddenly they heard the sounds of footsteps coming up the stairs. In a great panic they fled from their seats and rushed to lie under the floor. Ossie lay on his back in the dark and listened. His heart was pounding.

"Is who up here?" It was Maas Rashie. "Oonuh better talk fast! Mi mind tell me some idle boys under this floor you know. I heard some heavy sounds just now; no ratbat can make that kind of sound. Oonuh come out at once!" Ossie heard Maas Rashie's heavy footsteps pass right over him. Maas Rashie stomped on the floor. "Come out, you little rascals!" Nobody moved. Ossie heard him saying something about the wickedness of the young generation.

Then he went back down the stairs.

It was becoming difficult to breathe. Ossie felt his clothes sticking to his sweaty body. He wondered if the place was dirty and if it was soiling his clothes which he would have to wear to school. He began crawling backward towards the exit hoping to get some air.

A few moments after he lifted his head from the hatch he heard footsteps on the stairs again. Much to his annoyance he had to dive under once more. But these were the footsteps of people who wanted to watch the show from the balcony. There were now also the sounds of conversation and laughter. The balcony was quickly filling up.

The service which preceded the show began. They sang a number of songs including 'A Little More Oil In My Lamp' and 'Light Up The Corner Where You Are'. Then, with much gusto, they sang 'Rescue The Perishing', his mother's favourite hymn. He thought he could hear his mother's voice rising above everyone else's as they sang. He believed she was there, for she had had her dress on the bed ready to put on when he went into her room for the ten cents. If word got to the parson he would be sure to drag them out and shame them in front of the entire congregation. Then he would preach a sermon against them.

After the short service the lights went out for the film. One of the boys near him began whispering a message from Phonso – while it was dark they should emerge quietly one at a time.

Once again Ossie slowly worked his way back to the exit. But when he raised his head he found that the place was packed to capacity. The backs of people were only inches away from his face. There was no way he could get out without being detected. He had to remain there until the show was over. He slipped back under the floor to whisper a report on what he had seen. Then he returned to the edge of the exit and, with just enough of his face outside to enable him to breathe, he resigned himself to his fate. He would be unable to see the film. In addition to that, if detected he would be cruelly shamed.

He gathered from the sound of the film that it was based on the Bible story of Paul and Silas. They were imprisoned because of their religion. While in prison they prayed and sang psalms. This brought about a tremendous earthquake which burst open the prison and set them free. But if there should be an earthquake now, Ossie thought, his friends and himself were the ones most likely to be destroyed. They would be punished for their sins.

He slid under the floor again during the intermission. A collection was taken. Then they put out the light again and got ready for the second film.

This film didn't have much of a story. A male-voice choir sang beautifully harmonised choruses and the congregation joined in. The church was a happy place. Ossie sweated with unhappiness and remorse.

After the doxology people began leaving the church. Ossie waited until everyone had left the balcony and then he followed them quickly down the stairs. He wanted to get lost in the crowd. He heard the footsteps of his friends coming scampering down behind him.

Downstairs he kept close to the wall and avoided the light. He felt dirty with dust. Happily, he was soon out in the fresh air again.

One-Son caught up with him. "Man," he said with his voice barely above a whisper, "I could kill Phonso!"

"Where is Phonso?" asked Ossie.

"I don't know."

They looked around for him.

"See him there," said One-Son.

Phonso was at the edge of the crowd which surrounded the ice-cream vendor. The light of the vendor's torch shone on him. He held a laden ice-cream cone in each hand, and was hungrily licking first one and then the other alternately.

Brightly, Washie and Philbert joined them and they stood together watching Phonso without comment.

Then Ossie heard his mother's voice. She was calling his name, trying to find him. His throat went dry and he felt unable to move.

"Your mother calling you, Ossie," said Brightly.

He hurried towards her. She was standing in the middle of the churchyard and looking all around as she called. With his head bowed and heart pounding he walked up to her.

"Come home at once," she said. "I am not leaving you here to join up with bad company."

She started walking and, deeply worried, he followed her.

As they walked she talked about the films. They were beautiful films, she said, and she was glad she had been able to see them. She gave no indication that she knew anything about his crime. Usually she became silent when angry, but now she was in a talkative mood. He became increasingly worried about his clothes; they had seemed all right in the dim light of the church, but he had no idea what they looked like from behind. As she walked, his mother's shoes chomped the gravel with a familiar rhythm. He followed behind, his hands clutched nervously in his pockets.

Then she stopped and turned to him. They faced each other, but it was too dark for him to see the expression on her face.

"I hear that some hooligans didn't pay to get in," she said. "They hid somewhere up in the balcony. What unrighteousness! Stealing into God's own house! I hope you will never get mixed up in that kind of evil."

Each sentence drove Ossie deeper into the earth. Before he sank altogether, she finished what she had to say, turned and continued walking. He struggled with himself, regained the strength in his legs, and began following again.

That night he had difficulty falling asleep. When he did, he slept badly. He had nightmares in which he was chased by crowds, parsons and ratbats. And in each dream Phonso was in the front line of his pursuers.

The following morning, on his way to school, he hid the coin under a rock behind a bank. It was clear to him that he could not spend it; it was cursed money. He decided he would give it up as an offering at church the following Sunday. Three days later, he decided that, since he hadn't seen the films but only heard them, it was five cents that he actually owed. The following day he decided that he should pay a portion of the remainder as penance money. He dropped seven cents into the collection plate the following Sunday. It was six cents more than he usually contributed. Maas Rashie raised his eyebrows as he saw the coins rolling into the collection plate. He gave Ossie a piercing look, and without further comment moved on.

Baptism

One Sunday everyone noticed that Miss Daphne was absent from church. Her seat at the right end of the third row remained unoccupied throughout the service. While everyone filed out of the church at the end, Ossie overheard Miss Imogene, the old woman who usually sat beside Miss Daphne, discussing her with some of the other church members. They wondered if she was ill, or if some emergency had kept her away. It was unlike Miss Daphne to be absent from any service, and it was even more unusual for her to be absent on the first Sunday of the year. Miss Imogene said she would send one of her grand-children to Miss Daphne's home to find out how she was.

For some time now, Ossie had been observing Miss Daphne. She was fair-complexioned, aging, stony-faced, and she always wore a broad-rimmed white straw hat. She smiled only when the minister shook her hand after service, or when someone introduced her to a visitor. Her smile revealed her large upper front teeth, and the row of small compact ones at the bottom. Perhaps because it was such a contrast to her sphinx-like inscrutability, Ossie found her smile attractive. She seldom spoke, but when she did her voice was somewhat hoarse, although not unpleasantly so, and it had a child-like supplication tone which was a bit surprising in a fully grown woman. Her eyes, with their slight touch of hazel, were her most expressive feature – they were intensely searching, especially when listening to the minister preaching his sermon, and sometimes they seemed despairing, furtive and very afraid.

Ossie had heard it said that Miss Daphne was the leader of a straw-work cooperative which specialized in the making of hats and handbags for the tourist industry. She travelled a long distance to church, and passed many other churches on the way. She apparently had strong family ties with the church, for her surname was the same as many of those on the plaques on the church walls. The old-time people said the church was built during the time of slavery, and that some families could trace their membership back to those days; some of these, especially the mulatto families, had spearheaded the leadership in the church throughout most of its history. Miss Daphne, it seemed, belonged to one of these families. She held no office in the church – the church was no longer monopolized by mulattoes – but she was a devout follower of those who did lead.

Ossie had observed a peculiarity in Miss Daphne. Unlike the other grown-ups, she showed no interest in children. She did not seem to care whether they misbehaved or not. In fact, it occurred to Ossie that, although he attended church perhaps as frequently as she did, he could not recall a single occasion on which she had even looked at him.

The following Sunday, Ossie heard the reason for Miss Daphne's absence from church. During the break between Sunday school and the morning service he was standing at the foot of the steps to the main entrance. Miss Imogene and some other women were standing between the old tomb and the belfry, and Ossie could hear them discussing Miss Daphne.

"She went to the Baptist church," said Miss Imogene. "A friend invited her. And she heard Rev. Winston Burchell preach about baptism. He told them that baptism by immersion is necessary for salvation. He said Jesus chose the form of baptism practiced by John the Baptist, and that that was the form his followers should use. I hear it was a powerful sermon and it reached Miss Daphne. At the end of the service she offered up herself for baptism."

"What a thing, eh?" said a fat, round-faced woman in a white dress. "Imagine going from church to church in search of God."

"It don't look good at all," said a naseberry-complexioned woman with gold teeth. "It looks as if she is saying that our rector and our church can't save souls."

"Maybe she is getting crazy in her old age," said a shapely young woman who had only recently joined the church.

"Maybe it doesn't really matter," said the round-faced woman. "They say the church is one."

The Saturday night before the baptism, Ossie and his friends went to the Baptist church to look at the candidates. They peered through the windows and saw them sitting together in the first four rows with the rest of the congregation behind them. They were all dressed in white, and their heads were covered with white shawls. Ossie looked at the end of the third row in search of Miss Daphne but she was not there. He found her in the middle of the second row. She had both hands on her lap, and she was staring fixedly ahead at the altar as if concentrating on it. The lines of her face seemed softer in the light of the gas lamp and, in contrast with the predominantly black faces around her, hers seemed almost marble pink, merging into the white shawl surrounding it. Ossie was unable to see the expression in her eyes, but her general manner was one of resolution and quiet patience. For a few minutes Ossie and his friends listened to the choruses and revivalist hymns sung by the congregation.

"They are going to sing and pray all night," said Phonso. "In the morning the minister will come to lead the procession to the river." The following morning Ossie left home early to fetch water from the village tank but, since he had never seen a baptism, and regarded such a thing with a mixture of horror and fascination, he hid his zinc-pan in the bushes and decided to follow the procession to the river. He sat on the stone-wall and waited for the procession to arrive. While he waited he thought about this practice called baptism. He was glad that they did not require that kind of baptism at his church; he would not have liked having his head shoved under the water. There was something child-like in this submission to the will of the minister which he found surprising in grown-ups. They had christened him when he was an infant, and he was glad they had done it when he was too young to know what was happening. But there was something mysterious about this coming together of church and river which intrigued him. He felt that there must be something to it if people took it so seriously. There was a picture on the wall of the sitting-room at his home which represented the baptism of Jesus. It showed Jesus waist-deep in a river, with his hand clasped on his naked chest while he gazed up into heaven, and a gleaming white dove hovered above his head. Ossie had seen the picture all his life, but neither of his parents had ever spoken about it. He found the picture haunting and mysterious, and he knew now that its mystery had something to do with what was about to take place in the river in the valley.

Before long Ossie heard the procession approaching. He heard the people singing 'Onward Christian Soldiers'. Soon they came into view. The Rev. Winston Burchell led the procession. He was a fat, very black man and he held his head high; his expression was a mixture of righteousness and confidence. He clutched his hymn book and Bible close to his heart, and his black gown flowed behind him, rising slightly in the wind as he did a slow march to the rhythm of the hymn; he was singing the hymn fervently from memory. Behind him the candidates marched in pairs. They were followed by the well-dressed church members, and then by a disheveled band of onlookers, idlers and curiosity seekers. As they passed, Ossie watched for Miss Daphne. She was in the seventh row on the left. She held her open hymn book in front of her and was singing zestfully. Ossie waited until everyone had passed and joined the onlookers in the rear. Some of them were his friends, and they called to each other.

About half-a-mile on, the procession turned off the main road and began descending a winding side-road which led down into the eastern valley. From his position at the back, Ossie had a view of the procession as it meandered its way through the green cultivated fields and the open stretches of grassland. The pace was quicker now they were going downhill. As they approached the river they began singing, 'Shall We Gather at the River'.

Ossie squeezed his way forward as far as he could, until he was able to see what was happening. The place of baptism was a huge pool specially dammed up for the occasion with rocks and sand. Beside the river were two bamboo huts covered with coconut fronds which would be used as dressing-rooms. On the open land beside the huts, women were preparing a hot beverage over an open wood-fire.

The Rev. Winston Burchell stood with his back to the pool and faced the candidates, church members and onlookers who were now spread out in a fan-shaped congregation up the sloping bank of the river. He went through the preliminaries in his rich, booming voice, and then waded out to the centre of the pool which rose just above his waist.

When the shorter candidates waded into the pool to be baptized, the minister came out to meet them. But he had some difficulty with those who were taller or fatter than himself, and the church members resented it when a few chuckles came from the onlookers. Most of the candidates went down easily enough, and came up shouting ecstatic halleluiahs. One or two resisted and had to be shoved under several times in order to obtain the immersion which was required. One woman in particular clung to the minister with a firm hold.

"Duck her again, Parson!" shouted a woman behind Ossie. "Is wicked dem wicked when dem struggle so! Duck her again! One more time! Yeah!"

Ossie waited anxiously for Miss Daphne. When her turn came she waded out meekly with her head bowed and her palms clasped penitently under her chin. To Ossie's astonishment, she went under as smoothly as if she had a spine made of rubber, and she came up shouting such a flood halleluiahs that Ossie could feel the effect of her ecstasy run through the crowd.

"She found her Jesus at last," said a woman beside Ossie.

"Praise the Lord!" cried Miss Daphne, throwing both arms in the air. "Sing for me!" she requested. The congregation, which obviously had a special interest in her, responded with enthusiasm.

"When the roll is called up yonder. . ." they sang.

"I'll be there," responded Miss Daphne.

"When the roll is called up yonder ..."

"I'll be there," said Miss Daphne with tears of happiness.

"When the roll is called up yonder ..."

"We'll be there!" shouted Miss Daphne as she threw herself into the extended arms of her new church brothers and sisters.

To get to the dressing-room Miss Daphne had to pass Ossie. As she came close she stopped and looked straight into his eyes. It was clear that she recognized him as someone from her former church. She looked at Ossie as if he and his church were retreating into the distance. In her now joyous, hazel-tinged eyes, Ossie saw someone looking into a past from which she at last felt liberated.

She went into the dressing-room to put on the clothes for her first service of redemption.

After the baptism, Ossie began climbing the hillside path to the main road. He found himself walking behind two men in suits.

They conversed as they walked, and Ossie soon discovered that they were discussing baptism.

"Getting baptized is a way of saying something to the world," said the man in the blue suit. "You're saying that the outward cleansing by immersion resembles the inner state of being totally cleansed of sin."

"Is that what parson told you?" asked the man in the brown suit.

"Not just what parson said. It is something I have read about and thought out for myself. We are told that there must be a link between water and the spirit if we are to enter the Kingdom. So the rebirth in the water signifies the rebirth of the spirit."

Ossie passed them as he hurried to complete his chores. He recovered his zinc-pan and fetched three loads of water from the tank. As he carried the water on his head he thought of its importance for washing and other things. As far as he knew, water was the only thing that could cleanse, so that was perhaps why there had to be a link between water and spirit. But what was spirit? That he did not know.

Later that morning he went to his own church. The service was conducted by the Rev. Claude Silvera, the minister. He was dark-brown, with a broad face and he wore rimless spectacles. It seemed he had heard of Miss Daphne's story, for he preached about baptism. He said:

"We regard baptism as one of the important sacraments of the church. It is an outward sign of an inward grace. But it is the inward, spiritual grace, a gift of God, which is most important. The form of the outward sign – sprinkling, effusion, immersion – is of lesser importance. We christen infants because we believe children have a right to the spiritual benefits of the church. But we will offer immersion to unbaptised persons who wish it. Jesus never baptised anyone, neither did he specify the form that baptism should take."

Ossie thought of the joy he had seen in Miss Daphne's eyes, and of the learned confidence of his minister's voice. But to his mind, the mystery of the picture in the sitting-room at his home remained. Perhaps he would understand those things when he got older.

As the service progressed, he looked across and noticed that Miss Imogene had moved over to occupy Miss Daphne's former seat. She could now enjoy the coziness of the corner, and the comfort of an arm-rest during the long sermons. As the months went by Ossie noticed that there were no more references to Miss Daphne in their church.

The Sexton

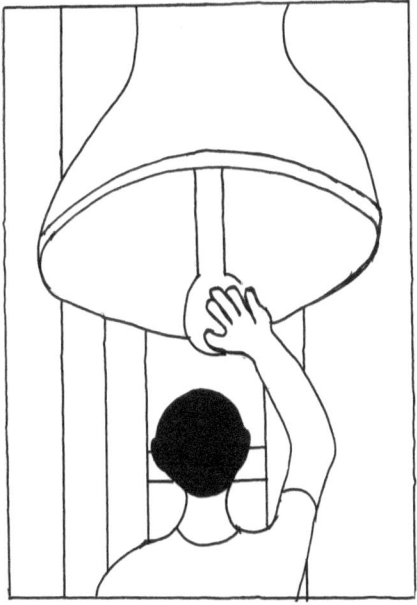

I t was close to noon and Ossie set off for the church property
to see if his goat was sheltered from the sun and if she needed
a change of feeding place. As he passed the house where the
sexton lived, the front door opened and Maas Rashie and Sister
Maudie came out.

"You can toll bell, Ossie?" asked Maas Rashie.

"What, sah?"

"Do you know how to toll the bell?"

"Toll it fi what, sah?"

"Brother Jonas is dead."

"Dead, sah?"

"Yes. Him took down sick suddenly last night and Sister Maudie
and myself decided to come across to see how him feeling. And

we just found him stiff dead in his bed. We going to get help. Climb up and toll the bell."

Maas Rashie and Sister Maudie started walking quickly down the hill.

"Is him alone in there, sah?" Ossie shouted after them.

"Yes," Maas Rashie replied. "But he is dead. Fear the living, son. Not the dead."

Ossie watched them as they crossed the churchyard below. At the gate they stopped and argued for a short while. Then they went their separate ways.

Ossie turned to look at the silent old wooden building. Somewhere inside there was a dead man lying on a bed. He shivered and felt his head seeming to expand. He turned again and looked across the churchyard, out to the road, in search of signs of the living. But there was no one in sight. He was alone with the quiet church below him, with the decaying wooden structure that sheltered old Jonas, with the motionless trees and grasses, and with the hot presence of a midday sun which soaked itself into the silent fact of death.

The bell hung from a branch of a mango tree at the other end of the yard, and could be reached by climbing the wooden ladder erected for that purpose. Ossie walked across the yard and shook the ladder to test it for firmness. He discovered that it was firmly planted in the earth and securely nailed to the tree. Brother Jonas took no chances with people who might want to steal his ladder. Ossie glanced at the silent house again and began climbing towards the bell.

To toll the bell, he had to grip the tip of the tongue and strike the ball against the side. For ordinary ringing Brother Jonas banged the bell from side to side. Ossie could see the two worn spots that had borne the brunt of years of ringing. No one but Brother Jonas ever rang that bell. He rang it three times on Sundays, and on weekdays when there were special meetings or services.

All his life Ossie had been used to hearing Brother Jonas ringing that bell. Everyone in the village was accustomed to his frantic rhythm. He helped create the religious mood of Sunday mornings. He was the people's clock as well as their constant reminder of the events of the church. His ringing of that bell was a village institution. Ossie could hardly believe that he was about to toll that same bell announcing the old man's death.

He gripped the tongue and made the first strike. The sound cut into his ears and he had to turn his head away and cover his ears with his hands. He wondered how Brother Jonas was able to stand it. No wonder the old man was slightly deaf. Perhaps he himself barely heard the peals he had sent echoing across the valleys year after year. Perhaps as the years went by he had grown so accustomed to those peals that he had stopped hearing them. He had learned to shield himself from the noise of informing other people.

After each stroke Ossie listened carefully to the sound as it gradually diminished. He looked across the valleys at the houses along the hillsides. Everywhere, people were listening to the tolling of the bell and wondering who had died. They were thinking of all the old and ill people they knew. Some had already heard about Brother Jonas from Maas Rashie and Sister Maudie. News travelled very quickly in the village. Those who had not yet heard were taking it for granted that it was Brother Jonas who was tolling the bell. The others were probably wondering who was tolling it now.

Ossie wondered if his mother was listening, and if his friends and acquaintances could imagine that he was the one sending those signals over the hills and valleys. Impressed with his own importance, he landed an exceptionally heavy stroke. He was at the centre of what was happening in the village.

But his thoughts soon returned to the old man. Brother Jonas lived alone. For more years than most people in the village could remember, he had taken care of the church building and the surrounding property, and performed various simple duties in exchange for the privilege of living in the old building and planting his crops on the available land.

He was short, black and very thin, and he walked with a jerky bounce. He wore a thick, cloth cap and was almost never seen without it. Children on their way from school teased him about taking it off. Everybody, young and old, at some time or other teased old Jonas. In spite of these torments, or perhaps because of them, he had developed a legendary patience and good humour.

But he was not without his fits of anger. Whenever people let their animals eat his crops, or mess up the churchyard, his seething anger would last for several days. On some of these occasions, the unforgiving violence of his wrath shocked even the most liberal-minded of his fellow church members. But, as far as was known, no one had ever succeeded in driving him to the point of using indecent language. His bitterest and most vicious pronouncements never went beyond the actual wording, or style, of the scriptures and the proverbial. Just about every word old Jonas cursed with could be found in the Bible. He used them out of context and gave them his own meanings, but what did that matter? The people got the point and he remained safe within the confines of the sacred scriptures.

Now as he tolled the bell, Ossie kept hoping that his goat hadn't escaped and destroyed any of the old man's crops. To toll the bell over his dead body and destroy his crops at the same time would be too much. He recalled that he had taken special care to measure the distance from the reach of his goat to the adjoining field of young banana suckers. And he had allowed a full yard between the goat and the field. Brother Jonas didn't allow too many people to tie their animals on the church property, but he had given Ossie special permission. Ossie remembered the event that had led up to the permission and, as he did so, the fear of destroying the old man's crops, on the very day of his death, sent a chill of impending remorse through his body. He was nervous as he took the tongue of the bell in his fingers, and the stroke he made was weak and apologetic.

One dark night some months before, while on his way to a political meeting in the village square, Brother Jonas stumbled and fell into a pit used by the village butcher for draining off the blood and excrement of slaughtered animals. The pit was foul and stinking.

Ossie happened to be passing at the time, also on his way to the meeting, and he heard the old man's cries. At first he had no idea where the sound was coming from. He stood still and listened. He heard an angry voice. He called out and the voice of old Jonas answered him from the pit. Carefully, he felt his way to the edge. By holding onto a nearby soursop tree with his right hand, and reaching down to the old man with his left, he managed, after considerable difficulty, to help him out. Brother Jonas' hands, feet and clothes were smeared with the foul- smelling excrement of the pit. But he had not lost his sense of humour as he said he had noticed that Ossie had not laughed at him.

Ossie recalled that this was true. He had not laughed. But he wasn't certain why he hadn't. Perhaps he was too frightened, or perhaps he was so anxious to catch what was left of the meeting he just wanted to pull the old man out as quickly as possible so he could be on his way. But his intervention had impressed the old man very much and he had gone around the village telling people about it. He said there were few boys in the village who would not have laughed at him. He went to Ossie's parents and told them they had a gentleman for a son. Ossie was embarrassed by all this praise.

A few days later, he was standing by the bank of a road trying to find a feeding place for his goat when Brother Jonas came by on his way to the square. He stopped and talked to Ossie and told him he could tie his goat on the church property anytime he liked. He only had to be careful, he said. Ossie didn't feel that he merited any special privileges just for helping the old man but, when it became difficult to find feeding places, he began taking up the offer. He realized, now, that the event had meant something important to Jonas, and he kept hoping that he had not broken his record of carefulness on the very day of the old man's death.

A few minutes later Maas Rashie returned with the village undertaker.

"Ok, Ossie!" he shouted up at him. "That is good enough. Come down now. You not as useless as I thought you were."

Ossie scrambled down the ladder. Maas Rushie and the undertaker were walking towards the house. Ossie followed them. At the door they stopped and turned to him.

"You better not come in, son," said the undertaker. "Wait until the funeral."

"Can't I just take a little peep, sah? I won't stay long."

"It's ok," said Maas Rashie. "Let him look for a minute if he wants to."

Maas Rashie pushed the door open and the undertaker and Ossie followed him. It was dark and stuffy inside. Maas Rashie walked across the room and opened a window. The light streamed into the bare, impoverished room. Brother Jonas lay on the bed with his face to the wall. He wore blue pyjama bottoms and a tattered merino. At first glance it seemed as if he was asleep. Only the sustained stillness conveyed the reality of death.

"Ok, Ossie," Maas Rashie said after a few moments. "That is enough."

Ossie closed the door behind him and walked out into the sunshine. His parents had taken him to several funerals and, like everyone else, he had joined the lines and looked at the powdered faces in the coffins. He didn't like funerals. The slow, mournful singing, the cries of weeping relatives, the final sound of clods of earth crashing down on the wooden coffins, all saddened and frightened him. Jonas looked as if he had fallen asleep and just hadn't bothered to wake up. Perhaps it was funerals that made death sad.

Then he remembered his goat and began sprinting towards the spot where he had tied her. He found the banana field reduced to shreds and spikes. The goat, full and satisfied, was lying in the shade of a nearby breadfruit tree peacefully chewing her cud. He felt tears stinging his eyes. With the tears already running down his cheeks he grabbed a piece of stick and, brandishing it angrily in the air, rushed with threats and sobs towards the waiting goat.

The Kite

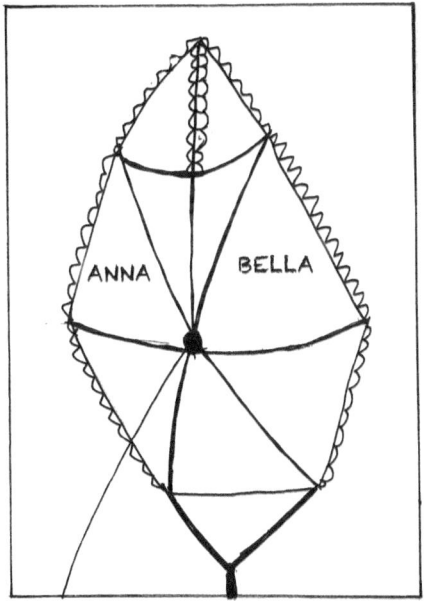

Mrs. Annabella Nelson, the stone-breaker, worked at the big corner in front of the village square near to the school. Ossie passed her each day on his way to and from school. Each time he would greet her, and she always gave him a cheerful reply. But beyond that they had never spoken to each other.

Ossie gradually became accustomed to the rhythm of her work. She collected big stones from a nearby hillside where they had cut a new road, and she carried the stones in an old bucket on her head. She began on the flat ground with only a few stones in front of her. Her pile grew gradually, and soon she was able to sit on top of it. Sitting on top of the pile, she broke the stones with her stone hammer and the pile grew under her until it was six or more feet high. Then a truck would come and they would buy the stones from her. Then she would start again with a small pile.

Mrs. Nelson and her husband lived in a wooden house near the Clear Water River. They had no children.

One morning Ossie was on his way to school, and he had a kite slung over his left shoulder. The kite was red, white and blue, and made of paper pasted with cassava starch onto a bamboo frame. The tail, which was made of bits of cloth tied together, was tied into a neat bundle.

"Good morning, Miss Anna," said Ossie as he passed the stone-breaker.

"Good morning, mi love. What a pretty kite you have! You made it?"

"Yes, ma'am."

"Bring it here – let me look at it."

Ossie walked towards her with the kite.

"What is your name, mi love?"

Ossie told her.

She took the kite from him and held it up to the light so she could admire the colours. Ossie noticed the contrast between the delicate kite and the stone-breaker's hard and calloused hands. She turned the kite around and admired it from different angles.

"You will be flying it after school?" she asked as she returned the kite to Ossie.

"Yes, ma'am."

"I will watch out for it from here. If you fly it from up the playfield I will be able to see it."

"Ok, ma'am. Gone, ma'am."

"All right, Ossie."

That evening, after school, Ossie headed for the playfield with his kite. He was followed by his friends, Washie and Brightly. They had no kites of their own and they wanted to help Ossie fly his. There was a brisk wind blowing from the north-east and, with his back to the wind, Ossie began hoisting his kite. At each stroke of his hand the wings of the kite buzzed in the wind. As the kite mounted, his roll of cord spun in the grass behind him.

Soon he was at the end of the cord, and he was holding the piece of rose-apple wood onto which the cord was tied. The colours of the kite shone in the evening sun. The kite was now surrendered to the pressure of the wind, settling over the village square. Sometimes it swayed gently to the right and sometimes to the left. When Ossie stroked the cord the kite mounted the sky. He put the cord to his ear and listened to the wings of the kite singing in the wind.

Ossie and his friends took turns in flying the kite. Then, when it was time to go, he began pulling it down by wrapping the cord onto the rose-apple stick.

Mrs. Nelson was still seated on her pile of stones when Ossie and his friends passed by later that evening.

"I could see your kite, Ossie," she called out to him. "It was beautiful in the evening sun. I sit here day after day breaking stones. But I just love to watch things that fly: aeroplanes, birds, kites. You plan to fly it again tomorrow?"

"Yes, ma'am."

"Good, mi boy."

"Gone, ma'am."

"Yes, mi love."

The following evening Ossie and his friends went to the play-field again with the kite. Ossie hoisted the kite and it settled over the village square. Once again his friends and himself took turns in flying the kite.

Then they were joined by a gang of big boys from the top class in the school. One of them, a stocky youth named Lloyd Perry, carried a kite which was more than three times the size of Ossie's. Lloyd Perry had a big grin on his face. He came close to Ossie and began hoisting his kite. The kite was so big that the wings made loud grunts each time he stroked it.

"Watch out, Ossie!" shouted Brightly. "His kite has razor blades on its tail!"

Ossie looked at the tail of Lloyd Perry's kite and, sure enough, the razor blades could be seen glistening in the sun. Ossie tried moving his kite away, but Lloyd Perry kept following him with his. The members of Lloyd Perry's gang began to laugh.

"Leave the boy's kite alone!" pleaded Washie.

"Pull in your kite, Ossie!" shouted Brightly. "Pull in your kite!"

Ossie began pulling in his kite as quickly as he could. But Lloyd Perry soon achieved his objective. He crossed Ossie's cord with his own, got the tail of his kite to rub against Ossie's cord, and then he stroked his kite to get it to move upwards. The razor blades cut Ossie's cord and Ossie's kite went limp. Ossie watched helplessly as the body of his kite sank towards its tail. Then it began drifting away into a distant south-western valley.

The members of Lloyd Perry's gang laughed and shook each other's hands.

"You taught the small-boy a lesson, Lloyd," said one of them. "You taught him never to fly his kite at the same place where the big boys fly theirs."

And they all laughed some more.

Without saying a word, Ossie tried to salvage as much of his cord as he could, but most of it had floated away with the kite. Then he went into the school, collected his bag, and began walking home. His friends Washie and Brightly walked with him.

Mrs. Nelson was still on her pile breaking stones. "I saw what happened," she said. "That other kite cut your cord."

"He did it on purpose," said Ossie.

"Who?"

Ossie told her.

"You just wait until I see him. Why he don't pick on boys his own size? Anyway, never mind, mi love. Go look for your kite. I think it is in Maas Rashie's yam field."

Ossie left Washie and Brightly and set off on a short cut down into the valley.

After searching for about half-an-hour he found the kite at the edge of Maas Rashie's yam field. It was perched on a yam stick and he used a bamboo pole to get it down. The paper was badly torn but the frame was still sound. He also managed to salvage more of his cord. It was getting dark when he set off for home.

He had homework to do that night so he put the kite away. He decided that he would repair it over the weekend.

The following morning he stopped at Mrs. Nelson's stone pile and talked to her about the kite.

"I am going to put razor blades on the tail," he said. "I am going to show that Lloyd Perry that he is not the only one who can cut down other people's kites. You just watch me and him!"

"Don't study revenge, mi son," said Mrs. Nelson. "Revenge is a bad thing. If you manage to cut down his kite, there will be two kites cut down instead of one."

"But he started it. And look what he did to mi kite."

"I understand your feelings. But there is nothing uglier than a kite with razor blades on its tail."

"What you mean, ma'am?"

"A kite is supposed to be a pure, beautiful thing flying in the sky. Razor blades spoil that."

"I think I see what you mean."

"Keep flying your kite, but fly it in the right spirit. Without razor blades."

"But people laughing at me because Lloyd Perry cut down mi kite."

"Ignore them. Besides, I don't think you going to have any more trouble with Lloyd Perry."

"Why not?"

"I talked to him earlier this morning. He passed here on his way to tie out his father's cow. I told him that if he cut down your kite again, he's going to have me to contend with as well. And I break stones for a living … I gave him a real cussing, and I told him the right and proper way to fly a kite."

"Thanks."

"But revenge is not the way."

"Ok gone, ma'am."

"All right, mi love."

The following Saturday evening, after completing his chores, Ossie settled down to repair his kite. He used a paste made from cassava starch to stick the paper onto the bamboo frame. This time he used red, yellow and white paper.

When he was finished he felt like giving his kite a name. He thought about it for a while but no suitable name came to his mind. He was about to put the kite away when the idea came to him. He would name the kite after Mrs. Nelson. But the name 'Mrs. Nelson' didn't sound musical enough. He thought her first name sounded better, so he named the kite 'Annabella'. He cut the letters out of blue paper and pasted them at the bottom of the kite. Then he hung the kite on a nail in the wall and left it to dry.

The following Monday morning he stopped in front of Mrs. Nelson's stone pile.

"Good morning, Miss Anna," he said.

"Good morning, Ossie. Your kite looks brand-new."

"It is the same frame with new colours."

"It looks nice."

"And I named it after you."

"What?"

Ossie held the kite in front of her so she could read the name.

"You little rascal!" She laughed with pleasure. "That is very nice."

That evening Ossie took his kite up to the playfield. Lloyd Perry and another boy were already there flying their kites. Ossie went between them and began hoisting his kite.

"Watch out for Ossie!" one of Lloyd Perry's friends shouted to him. "He might cut down your kite!"

Lloyd Perry began moving out of the reach of the tail of Ossie's kite.

"No need to worry," said Ossie. "I don't keep razor blades on my kite. The air is free. It is for everybody."

"No more razor blades on mine either," said Lloyd Perry.

The other two kites were already hanging over the village square. Ossie fed his kite with cord so that it gradually mounted the air to join the others. Soon the 'Annabella' was swaying gently, its colours pure and beautiful in the sky.

Ripe Bananas

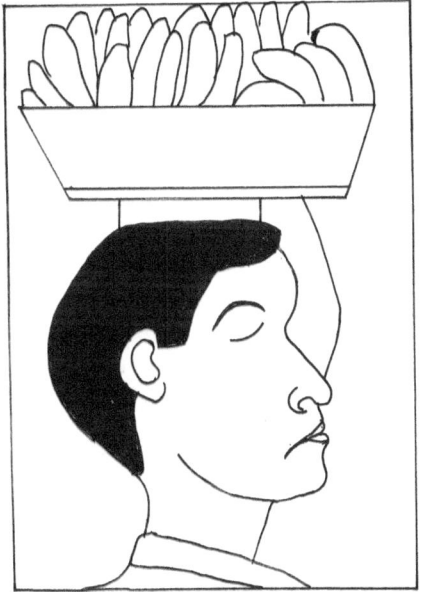

Ossie's father brought home a beautiful bunch of Gros Michel bananas from his field. The fingers were smooth and full and had the clear-green colour that bananas had when they were fit. He hung the bunch on a rafter in the kitchen and left it to ripen. Gradually the green fingers turned yellow, and soon they had a whole bunch of ripe bananas.

Ossie's mother was in the kitchen preparing supper, and she called Ossie in the house and asked him to bring the bottle of coconut oil. She was making fried dumplings. Ossie took the bottle to her.

"Ossie," she said after she took the bottle, "I want you to sell these ripe bananas at school tomorrow."

Ossie whined in protest. "They will laugh at me," he said.

"Don't be silly."

"Only women supposed to sell those things. Higglers sell bananas. I don't want to be a higgler."

"Don't Maas Trevor sell things, including bananas, in his shop? And isn't he a man?"

"But he doesn't carry things on his head and walk about and sell them."

"Do you know that there are men higglers in Kingston? Some of the biggest higglers are men."

"But that won't stop them from laughing at me."

"Listen, boy," said his mother, getting heated, "are you ashamed to earn decent money? We earn money by growing and selling things. If we don't sell things we will have no money to buy food and clothes, we will have no money to buy your books, or to give you lunch money to go to school."

Ossie sulked some more but said nothing. He thought of the women vendors who sold things in the schoolyard. They would probably see him as a competitor. He had, of course, seen male vendors passing through the village. They sold ice-cream, meat, and cloth for men's clothing. But he had never seen a man selling fruits.

"I will put the bananas in a tray," said his mother. She turned and looked into his eyes. "No horse should be ashamed to carry his own grass," she said. Then she began frying the dumplings. The following morning, it was with a heavy heart that Ossie left the house with the tray of ripe bananas on his head. He walked slowly so that his friends would get to school ahead of him; he did not want them to see him. He met a man riding a donkey down the hill.

"Hurry up, boy," said the man. "You will be late for school and teacher will beat you."

When Ossie arrived at school he found the schoolyard empty. Everybody was inside and it seemed as if classes were already underway. Ossie hoped the headmaster would not punish him and add to his discomfort. He entered through a side door and walked past another class on his way to his own. He felt the eyes of everyone on him. At his class he lifted the tray from his head and placed it on top of the cupboard.

"What a way the bananas pretty," grinned Phonso from his seat.

"I want a finger for free," said Washie.

Ossie squeezed his way into his seat.

"Are you selling those bananas, Ossie?" asked Mr. Llewellyn from his desk.

"Yes, sir."

"How much are you selling them for?"

Ossie told him.

"Please sell me a hand."

Ossie picked the biggest and most beautiful hand and took it up to his teacher. "Thank you, sir," he said as he put the money Mr. Llewellyn gave him into his pocket. He returned to his seat.

"These are Gros Michel bananas," said Mr. Llewellyn to the class. "The words 'Gros Michel' are French and mean 'Bid Michael'. This kind of banana was imported from another Caribbean island by the name of Martinique in 1835. It was imported by a French botanist and planter named Jean Pouyat and was first planted right here in this parish, from where it spread throughout the island and overseas to Central America. It has been known by many names, including 'Martinik', 'Pouyat', 'Whitehouse' and 'Go Yark', meaning 'Go to New York for you are the best'. It was the basis of our banana trade for a long time before being almost completely wiped out by Panama Disease. It is rarely found today and is in great demand. It is generally regarded as the most delicious banana ever grown here."

The students turned to look at Ossie who had inspired this unexpected history lesson. A girl in front turned round and smiled at him. Ossie felt grateful to Mr. Llewellyn.

"I am dying for recess time to come so I can taste those bananas," said a boy behind him.

At recess time Ossie found himself the most popular boy in the school. His friends sat with him on the wall beside the school-yard; they wanted to share his glory and the leftover bananas that Ossie said he would give away at the end of the day. Children crowded around him to buy the bananas. A few teachers, who had heard about the bananas from Mr. Llewellyn, came to buy hands to take home to their families.

By lunch time most of the bananas were sold. Ossie changed his mind about waiting until the end of the day before sharing the remaining bananas with his friends; he gave some away before they were all sold. He made sure to give one to the girl who had smiled at him.

After school Ossie began walking with his friends. He carried the empty tray on his head. The money jingled in his pocket as he walked; he had never carried so much money on his person before.

"Does your father have any more of those bananas?" asked Phonso.

"I don't know."

"Tell him to plant more, man. Look how quickly people bought them up."

When Ossie arrived home he found his mother and father sitting on the verandah. His mother was sewing and his father was slumped over the chair looking very tired after his day in the fields. Ossie greeted them and they returned his greeting. He put the tray away, took the money from his pocket and gave the notes and coins to his mother. His mother thanked him and counted the money.

"You did well, man," she said. "This is more than the higglers would have given us. And here is some pocket money for you."

Ossie took the money she gave him and smiled with pleasure.

"Did anybody laugh at you?" asked his mother.

"I didn't see anybody laughing."

"If you want something," his mother said, "why should it matter whether it is being sold by a man or a woman?"

"They seemed happy to buy the special bananas," said Ossie. He turned to his father. "Do you have any more of those bananas Papa?"

"Only suckers now," said his father. "But they will grow quickly. I am going to nourish the breed. I got the first sucker from a man at Greenvale. He said he got the breed from his grandfather."

Ossie sat on the wall of the verandah.

"Do you know what the words 'Gros Michel' mean?" he asked.

"No," said his father.

"No, I don't," said his mother. "That is why we send you to school. So that you can find out these things."

Ossie repeated the things his teacher had told the class.

His mother's eyes twinkled. "You must be the most learned vendor in the country today," she said.

And his mother and father laughed together.

Mango Ridge

The teachers were putting pressure on the students, for it would soon be the dreaded Inspection Day. The status of the school depended on how the students performed for the inspector. Some teachers had added evening classes to their timetable, and a few were even holding classes on Saturday mornings. Ossie's teacher was one of those holding extra classes. Ossie studied so hard that the time came when he felt he could do no more.

One Wednesday morning when he woke up, he was so tired he could not get out of bed. The thought of going to school depressed Ossie. He did not want to think of words and numbers, blackboard and chalk, pen and ink, ruler and books. He did not want to stand in lines, sit in a cramped row of desks, live in the constant fear of punishment. When he thought of the cross inspector and his difficult questions his palms sweated. He turned onto his stomach and pulled the sheet over his head.

A few minutes later, Ossie heard his mother's footsteps as she came into the room.

"Wake up Ossie!" she said. "Time to get up."

Ossie pulled the sheet from his face.

"I am not going to school today, ma'am."

"What is the matter? You sick?"

She felt his cheeks and neck with the back of her hand.

"I am tired," said Ossie. "The work is getting too hard. I want to sleep."

"Stay in bed then," said his mother. "I think we have enough water in the barrel. And I will tie out your goat for you later. I will leave your breakfast on the table."

Ossie slept late into the morning. When he woke up again he saw patterns of sunlight on the ceiling. It was the first time he had seen those patterns; he had never slept so late before. He put on his yard clothes, washed, and then sat down to the luxury of a leisurely breakfast. The house was very quiet and he realized he was alone there. Ossie nibbled his roast yam and saltfish and poured himself hot bissy from the thermos. Then he sat on the verandah and looked out at the sunlit yard and garden. So this is what the yard looks like at this time of day, he thought; he felt he was seeing it for the first time.

Ossie decided that later on he would collect feeding – mostly Spanish needles and thistles – for his rabbits. Then he would bathe at Falling Waters, a waterfall about half-a-mile away and the usual bathing place for males in the village. Later in the evening he would go and sit on the village stonewall and watch the life of the road.

But right now, Ossie just wanted to lie on the grass in his favourite spot and look over at the village of Mango Ridge. He left the house and followed a path downhill until he came to a patch of soft, inviting grass. At the centre was a bamboo clump which provided shade. The patch was almost surrounded by navel-orange trees which were laden with fruit. Ossie stretched out on the grass and looked across the valley at Mango Ridge.

Mango Ridge was near enough for him to see tiny-looking people and hear faint sounds. But although he had known of the village all his life, he had never been there. The left side of the ridge was higher than the right, and in the evenings he could see people walking on top of it on their way home. He could see their bodies in silhouette: men riding donkeys; men driving cows and goats in front of them; men and women with loads on their heads; and children following the grown-ups. They would disappear behind a hill, and he would wait to see them reappear on the backbone of the lower ridge. Ossie wondered what it was like at the back of the hill where they all disappeared. At Mango Ridge the red roads seemed smoother than those he knew; the houses formed more interesting patterns against the hillside; this village seemed a part of the large fascinating mountain in the east. In fact, Mango Ridge seemed an altogether more mysterious and interesting village than his own.

Ossie decided to visit Mango Ridge. He set off downhill, went through his father's yam field and banana cultivation, and then through a patch of guinea grass until he reached the river. As he waded across, he delighted in the cold water on his bare feet, and he laughed as he slipped on the slippery stones. Then, he was on the other side, at the foot of Mango Ridge.

He found a winding path which took him through the thick, lonely bushes, past a sweet potato field, and to the side of a large bamboo clump. The sight of the thick coverings – called 'jackets' – which fell from the joints of the bamboo shoots stirred a creative urge in him, and he decided to make a windmill. Using his penknife Ossie made a propeller from one of the jackets, and he attached it to the end of the bamboo stem. It was cool and pleasant in the shadow of the ridge, and he became aware of the pleasant smells of the cut bamboo, fever grass, and ripening plums on a tree he could not see. Ossie began whistling happily as he turned a bend and found himself on a stretch of land lined with blue flowers and ginger lilies. When he reached the top of the left of the ridge Ossie turned around and, for the first time, saw his home village of Clifton from afar. Most of the houses were nestled near the top of the long green hill which curved with an awesome beauty against the clear blue sky. Ossie gasped; he had no idea he lived in such an enchanting place. He recognized the main road, and his eyes moved downwards in search of his home. When he found it, it was just a patch of white partly concealed by the vegetation. This and his father's field below, he thought, were all that the people of Mango Ridge could see of his home. But now that he was looking up at it, he felt that his own village was far more imposing than Mango Ridge.

Ossie began running along the quiet road with the propeller of his windmill spinning in the wind. The road sloped suddenly downhill. Ossie ran through a fern-covered gorge. The sounds of insects buzzed in his ears. He came out of the gorge and on his left he saw a valley so deep that the thought of falling into it made him feel weak at the knees. He ran on while he watched the windmill turning in the wind.

"Stop!" said a man's voice.

Ossie stopped and looked ahead. There was a man standing in the road about twenty-five yards away. The man seemed naked at first, but Ossie saw that he was wearing dark swimming trunks. His body was covered with bees and some bees buzzed around it.

"Don't come too close," said the man. "The bees might sting you."

"Then why don't they sting you?" asked Ossie.

The man laughed. "I know how to stop them," he said. "I rub my body with certain combinations of weeds. My father taught me. This knowledge has come down in my family for generations."

"So what are you doing with the bees?" asked Ossie.

"I am taking them to a hive. This is the queen bee," he said holding up the bee he held between his thumb and forefinger. "Where the queen goes they will all go. I know how to control them. I am taking them about a mile from here."

"Any ever sting you yet?"

"Never. Go up on the bank so I can pass."

Ossie climbed the bank and watched the bees-man as he continued his way up the road. He watched him until he was out of sight. Then he continued running along the road with his windmill.

At the bottom of the hill he saw a fat woman bending over some produce at the side of the road. She was packing yams, sweet potatoes and breadfruits into a basket. She wore a white head-tie and an apron. As Ossie approached she stood up straight and turned to him.

"Don't talk to me," she said in a monotonous voice. "I am deaf Nenen and I can't hear anything you say. With me, talking is a one-way street. I can talk to people as much as I like, but I don't have to listen to them. They have to listen to me though and I can't hear their revenge. I don't have to listen to another hot word for the rest of my life. I wasn't born deaf and I remember the voice of the grandmother who raised me. I remember music as well, and I remember how the birds used to sing, but now my life is like the old moving pictures without sound. I live in total silence. You can't imagine that? You can hear, can't you?"

"Yes, ma'am," said Ossie.

Nenen returned to packing the produce into the basket.

Ossie continued running along the smooth red road. The road was now flat and lined with houses. There were hedges made from hibiscus and crotons.

As Ossie approached a white wooden gate on the left he heard the sound of a sweetcup whistle. He saw a boy of his own age standing behind the gate and looking out on the road. The boy had large eyes and his hair was parted on the left. He was calmly blowing his whistle. *Pu-pu-tuweetu!* When the boy saw Ossie he stopped blowing the whistle and beckoned for Ossie to come over to him.

"I am Syl," said the boy as he opened the gate. "Come, let me show you my animals."

Ossie followed Syl up the walkway. There was a white house with a zinc roof, glass windows and a small verandah. Syl led Ossie behind the house to a yard surrounded by cages.

"This is my little zoo," said Syl.

He showed Ossie a hutch with rabbits and guinea pigs. Ossie had never seen so many varieties of these animals. There were white rabbits, grey rabbits, and multi-coloured rabbits. There were smooth and ruffled guinea pigs. The rabbits stared placidly and the guinea pigs squealed hungrily.

"This is my dove house," said Syl.

There was a cage with barble doves, pea doves, ground doves and baldpates.

"And this is Sly, my pet mongoose," said Syl.

Ossie looked at the caged mongoose with interest. Most people hated mongooses because they stole chickens. But here was someone who loved them.

Syl then showed Ossie his fish tank. He said most of the fish came from rivers. The goldfish were gifts from relatives who lived in Kingston.

"I would love to get a crocodile," said Syl. "I want to get as many animals as I can."

He then took Ossie on a tour of the rest of the yard and showed him his ducks and guinea chicks.

"Why do you collect so many animals?" asked Ossie.

Syl's large eyes beamed.

"I want to become a zoologist when I grow up. I am sickly and I have to stay home for long periods so I study my animals here. You want a swap?"

"Swap what?"

"You give me your windmill and I give you a guinea pig."

"Sure," said Ossie giving Syl the windmill.

Syl went to the hutch and took out a mostly white guinea pig with a brown pattern over its haunches. "It is a male," he said as he placed it in Ossie's hands.

"Thanks," said Ossie looking into the vitality of its bright eyes.

After he left Syl, Ossie took a different path and began his descent to the river. He held the guinea pig gently on his chest, and he could feel its feet clutching his shirt. From time to time he stopped and stroked its sleek body. He also stopped to admire a jackfruit, which was bigger than the trunk of the tree on which it grew, to take note of the first starapple tree he had ever seen that bore fruits with pointed tips, and to marvel at a rock he saw on the river bed which was the shape of Jamaica.

He did not cross the river to land owned by a wealthy man they nicknamed 'Razor', for it was rumoured that Razor had planted sharp pegs on his land to injure trespassers. While Razor's neighbours lost their crops to thieves, his produce ripened and rotted in his fields. Ossie followed the river bed until he was able to cross over to his father's land.

When he arrived at his favourite spot, Ossie sat on the grass and looked over at Mango Ridge. Now he knew what it was like to walk and run on that red earth. He knew what was behind the hill where the people disappeared. The residents there were no longer mere silhouettes on the road: he knew something of the world of the bees-man, deaf Nenen and Syl. He also knew what the inhabitants of Mango Ridge saw when they looked at his home and his village.

"Ossie! Ossie! Where are you?"

It was his mother's voice.

"I am coming, ma'am!"

"Come for your lunch. You know how long I have been calling you?"

Ossie went to his rabbit hutch and put his guinea pig inside. The guinea pig hesitated for a few moments, then ran towards the rabbits, turned around and looked at Ossie. Two of the rabbits hopped about while the others stared indifferently.

"I am going to call you Mango Boy," said Ossie to his guinea pig. "And I am going to save up and get a wife for you."

As he walked towards the house he thought about his friends at school. He knew they would be wondering why he was absent. Perhaps his teacher had asked them about him, for it was not like Ossie to miss school; he prized the blue ink marks which were put in the attendance register when he arrived early, and the year before he had won a prize for his attendance record.

Ossie's friends were now probably buying their lunch from the vendors in the schoolyard. They were buying cornmeal pudding, gizzadas and totoes. He was not there to play gig with them during the lunch break. In the afternoon the boys would work in the school garden while the girls sewed. Ossie now felt nostalgia for his friends and the life of the school, and he wanted to go back. He was looking forward to the following day when, at recess time, his friends would gather around him to ask about his day off. He would tell them about Mango Ridge and his day of peace and freedom. By then he would feel refreshed and ready to resume preparations for the inspector.

In the meantime, there was more to come in Ossie's day yet. He was hungry after his journey, and he was hoping his mother had a delicious lunch waiting for him. After eating, he planned to pick the first feeding for his new friend Mango Boy and feeding for his rabbits too. Then there was the pleasure of Falling Waters with its three levels of pools which he could climb up to. He would feel its ice-cold water pounding his body. At the end of the day, broadened by his experience of Mango Ridge, Ossie anticipated sitting on the stone wall and watching new aspects of the life of his own village unfold in front of him.

The Reading Tree

It was a Friday afternoon and, after completing his chores, Ossie put a novel in his school bag, slung the bag over his left shoulder, and set off for his reading tree. He followed a winding path down the hillside, and then he turned off on a side track to his left. The track led him to the foot of a paper-skin mango tree. He climbed the tree with deft and well-practised movements.

In a few moments he arrived at his reading spot. The fork of the tree curved and made a comfortable seat. After completing the curve the branch sloped downwards and provided a convenient spot on which to rest his book. Ossie sat in this natural seat, took the novel from his bag, and hung the bag on a nearby stump. Then he settled down in the notch of the tree.

But before he started reading he looked around. He also liked the things he could see from his perch. There were blossoms on the mango tree on which he sat and also the nearby guinep and ackee trees. Below him were yellow, green and black cocoa pods on the cocoa trees. He watched as a banana quit flew from the branch of an orange tree and settled on a bare branch of a plum tree. In the distance he could hear a pea dove cooing and, on a nearby hillside, he could see rows of freshly-dug yam hills. Beyond the hills, the top of a blue mountain was hidden by floating white clouds.

Then he turned to the novel. It was the seventh one he would read on his reading tree. He had discovered the tree a few months before and it had become his secret hideaway from the world. Here, he explored other worlds, described in the books he borrowed from the school library.

One night, a few weeks later, Ossie was alone in the sitting room. It was after supper and he didn't feel like doing anything. He sat in the rocking-chair and rocked. His mother and father were on the verandah, and he could hear them talking. They were discussing how hard times were.

"It is getting hard to find wood," his father said.

"Yes," his mother agreed.

"I am thinking of cutting down a tree."

"Which one?"

"A mango tree. We have plenty of them."

Ossie stopped rocking and listened more attentively.

"Which mango tree?" his mother asked.

"The one just down the bottom. The one beside the ackee tree and the guinep tree."

"No!" shouted Ossie, springing to his feet.

He opened the door and went out to the dark verandah.

"No, Papa!" he pleaded. "Don't cut down that tree!"

"Why not?" asked his father.

"It is my reading tree."

"Your what?"

"I read and study in that tree."

"You read and study in a tree? What kind of thing is that? Don't you have the whole house to yourself to read and study? Why you have to study in a tree?"

"I just like the tree, Papa," said Ossie. "It is a nice place to read."

"Well, the land is full of trees," said his father. "You can always find another one. If that is where you want to study. What a place to choose!"

"But no tree will be as nice as this one," said Ossie. "Why don't you cut down another tree?"

"This tree is the nearest one to the house. We won't have to carry the wood too far. Besides, we have more than one paper-skin mango tree."

"I don't mind carrying the wood from far," said Ossie.

"That is what you are saying now. But I have to carry the wood too."

"It isn't good to cut down trees," insisted Ossie. "Teacher says that trees cause rain."

"We going to cut down only one tree," his father said. "And we need that wood to cook food. Wood is a necessity. And you can find a hundred places to read."

Ossie left the verandah and went into his room. He threw himself onto his bed. His father was bent on killing a tree that he had come to love. But Ossie was determined to fight him to the end.

The following morning he appealed to his mother. She was in the front yard, putting an enamel plateful of nutmegs in the sun to dry. Ossie admired the intricate patterns of brown and orange formed by the nutmegs. His mother bent to put the plate of nutmegs on the ground, then straightened up.

"Talk to Papa for me," said Ossie as he looked into her eyes. "Tell him not to cut down that tree."

"You know your father," his mother said. "Once he puts his mind to a thing, trying to change it is like bending iron."

"But maybe if you talk to him he will listen."

"I will try, but don't have any high hopes."

It was the end of the Easter break and school reopened the following Monday. It rained heavily after lunch. The school was a long one-room building divided into classrooms by chalkboards. The sound of the water on the roof combined with the noise of the children's voices made it very difficult for the teachers to teach. Ossie's class teacher, Mr. Llewellyn, wrote an assignment on the chalkboard. All pupils were asked to write compositions on topics of their own choosing. They were to hand in the compositions for correction as soon as they were finished.

Ossie wrote a composition entitled 'My Reading Tree'. The composition began with the following words: 'One of my best friends is neither a person nor an animal. It is a tree.' This tree, he went on, not only bore big juicy mangoes, it had the coziest reading spot he knew. He described the shape of the tree, the patterns of its branches, the smell of its bark and leaves. He listed the books he had read on his reading tree, and he listed the books he was still hoping to read. 'Now the life of my reading tree is threatened,' he concluded. 'It is to be felled by my father's own hand.'

Ossie picked up his exercise-book and carried it to Mr. Llewelyn's desk. Mr. Llewellyn had a round head and his hair was parted on the left. He read Ossie's composition and as he read he made correction marks with a red-ink pen. When he had finished reading he put a big tick in the left-hand margin. Then he looked up and gave Ossie a penetrating stare.

"Is it true what you wrote?" he asked Ossie.

"Yes, Teacher."

"Would you like me to have a word with your father about it?"

"Oh yes, Teacher."

"All right. I will."

"But do it soon, sir. Before he cuts down the tree."

"I will keep your book. Go back to your seat and read."

That evening after school Ossie ran all the way home. The first thing he did after he arrived was to go down the hillside to see if the tree was still standing. The tree was there, looking washed and green after the afternoon rain.

Later, at about five o'clock, Mr. Llewellyn arrived at the front of the house. Ossie was sitting alone on the verandah. Mr. Llewellyn hadn't bothered to change; he was still in his work clothes. He had Ossie's exercise book in his hand.

"Good evening, Mr. Johnson!" he called.

"Papa isn't here yet, sir," said Ossie, standing up.

"But is your mother here?"

"Yes, Teacher."

Ossie went to the back door and called to his mother who was in the kitchen.

"Teacher is here to see you," he said.

Ossie's mother fixed her head-tie and wiped the charcoal marks from her face. Then she went to the front of the house.

"Oh! Is Teacher Llewellyn!" she said.

"It is really your husband I want to see," said Mr. Llewellyn, "but maybe I could talk to you as well."

"He is not here right now, but I am expecting him back at any time. Please have a seat on the verandah and wait. I will soon come to you, Teacher."

She went back to the kitchen.

Mr. Llewellyn sat on the verandah beside Ossie. He began looking through the exercise book as he re-read all the earlier exercises.

"You like writing compositions," he said to Ossie.

"Yes, Teacher."

Ossie's father arrived a short while later. He entered the yard carrying a big basket on his head. He lifted the basket from his head and put it on the ground. It contained yam heads, some of which already had short vines growing.

"Hello, Teach!" he said to Mr. Llewellyn.

"Good evening, Mr. Johnson," said Mr. Llewellyn as he went out into the yard. "You are a strong man to be carrying so many yam heads."

"What to do, mi dear sah? The work must be done."

The two men shook hands.

"I see that you and Mrs. Johnson are very busy right now," said Mr. Llewellyn, "but I would like to talk to both of you for a few minutes. It won't take too long."

Ossie's father gave Ossie a penetrating and questioning look, as if he was wondering if Ossie was in some kind of trouble at the school.

"Call your mother, Ossie," his father said.

Ossie went to the back door.

"Papa is here!" he called to his mother. "They say you must come now."

"I am coming."

Ossie took two chairs from the sitting-room to the verandah. The small verandah could barely hold the four of them.

Ossie noticed that both his mother and father seemed worried.

When they were all seated Mr. Llewellyn opened the exercise-book.

"I am going to read for you," he said. "It is a composition that Ossie wrote today."

He read in a clear and well-modulated voice. To Ossie's ears, the composition sounded better when Mr. Llewellyn read it. When he had finished reading, Mr. Llewellyn turned to Ossie's father and then his mother.

"It is a fine composition," he said. "The boy is writing well. And he is writing well because he is reading well. He is one of the good readers in class. It is clear that the tree means a lot to him. If it is encouraging him to read this is a good thing. I think you should think carefully before you cut it down."

"I never thought the tree really meant that much to him," said his father.

"That tree is a tree of knowledge to the boy," said Teacher Llewellyn.

"In that case, I won't cut it down," said Ossie's father. "I will cut down one of the others."

Ossie grinned with pleasure.

"Thank you, Teacher," he said, "and thank you, Papa."

Teacher Llewellyn rose to go.

"You continue to work hard at your studies," he said as he handed the book to Ossie.

Then he shook hands with Ossie's father and mother.

"Thanks for your interest," said Ossie's father.

"We appreciate your visit," said Ossie's mother.

"Goodbye," said Teacher Llewellyn as he walked out into the yard.

After Teacher Llewellyn left, Ossie ran down the winding path and turned into the track that led to the tree. He hugged the trunk of the tree and patted it with the palm of his hand.

"You are going to live!" he said. "You are going to live!"

Wet Sugar

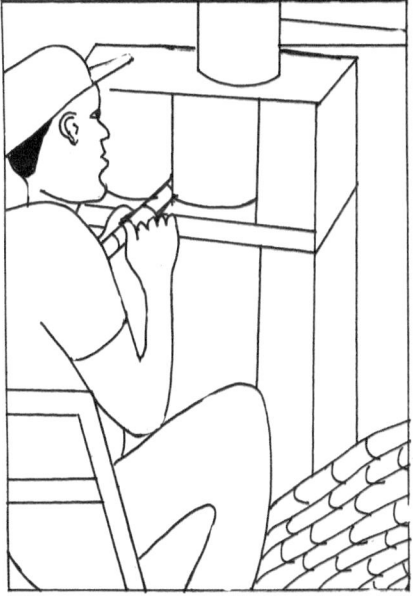

It was Saturday morning and Ossie wanted to spend most of the day at his Uncle Tony's sugar mill. He completed all his morning chores early and then, with his mother's permission, he set off for the mill. This would be his first visit to a sugar-mill and he was curious about what he would see.

Sometimes he walked and sometimes he ran, and he arrived at the mill about half-an-hour later.

The mill was a busy place. Men with bundles of sugar-cane on their heads were arriving from the cane-fields and piling up the cane at a corner of the mill-yard; then they returned to the cane-fields for more. The mill that crushed the cane was on a wooden stand at the centre of the yard. A man named Maas Eggie was the mill-feeder; he sat beside the mill and fed lengths of cane into it. The long wooden arm of the mill was drawn by a mule; the mule's hoof-prints made a circle close to the edge of the yard. The cane juice from the mill flowed in bamboo gutters and pipes down to the boiling-house which was a few yards further down the hillside. Ossie went down to the boiling-house to see what was happening there. There was a furnace under the boiling-house, and a man feeding it with wood and the left-over trash from the crushed canes. Inside the boiling-house they were boiling the cane juice in large coppers. They boiled off the liquid and the sugar settled at the bottom of the coppers.

But it was the mill crushing the cane that fascinated Ossie most of all, so he returned to the mill-yard to watch Maas Eggie do his work.

"Can I help you feed the mill?" asked Ossie.

"This is dangerous work, boy," said Maas Eggie. "The mill could pull your hand right in. Pass me cane from the heap if you want to work."

Ossie began carrying cane from the heap to the mill. Maas Eggie was a cheerful man who loved telling stories. He wore a brown, cloth cap and khaki shirt and pants. He had brawny arms. He split a fat cane with his machete so that the mill could receive each piece more easily. Then he said, "Your grandfather played a role in the erection of this mill."

"My grandfather? Which one?"

"Your father's father. 'Hercules' we used to call him. He was one of the strongest men in these parts."

"What did he do?"

"That is quite a story, mi boy. The man who built this mill was the owner before your Uncle Tony bought it. That man bought this iron mill in Kingston, and he brought it back to the square in a truck. Then the following day he went to the square with his cart to carry the mill down here. But nobody could lift the mill onto the cart. Several men tried lifting it together and they could barely raise it off the ground. The owner started saying he would have to pull it down and reassemble it here.

"Hercules, your grandpa, was with some other men in the bar drinking rum, and they were watching the men trying to lift the mill. Then, at somebody's suggestion, the men in the bar pooled together and bought a bottle of rum, and they said the rum would go to the man who could lift the mill onto the cart. Many of the men turned to your grandpa because they knew he was a strong man. But he just smiled and said, 'All a oonuh gwaan and try. If nobody can lift it, then I will try.'

"Hercules watched as man after man tried to lift the mill, but none of them could get it onto the cart. After everybody tried in vain, Hercules drained his glass, then he got up slowly and walked out into the square. He looked at the mill and he looked at the distance between the mill and the cart. There was a look of deep concentration on his face. It was as if nothing else existed in the world except himself, the mill and the cart. Then he bent down and gripped the mill. Every muscle in his body moved as he lifted the mill to right above his waist. Then he got under it, and with one big push the mill was on the cart.

"The men rushed out of the bar and lifted your grandpa in the air. Shouting and cheering, they carried him back to the bar and presented him with the bottle of rum. He opened the bottle and poured a drink for every man in the square. Then they had a big celebration. Your grandpa travelled with the cart down here to help them unload the mill. And after they built this stand, he was the one who lifted the mill to where it is now. So it is because of your grandpa why I am here today feeding this mill."

Ossie felt very proud of his grandfather. He said, "When I grow up I am going to be as strong as my grandpa."

"You have a good man to imitate," said Maas Eggie with a laugh. Ossie began to admire the men who were carrying the bundles of cane to the mill-yard. They entered the yard one at a time, lifted the bundles from their heads and threw them onto the heap. Some of them were wet with perspiration. They worked silently and seldom spoke.

Ossie decided that he would join them and help in carrying the cane from the cane-fields. He left Maas Eggie and began following Maas Eric, one of the men who carried cane from the fields. Maas Eric was lean and strong and he had a few days' growth of hair on his face. After a few minutes he turned to Ossie and said, "You want to carry cane?"

"Yes, sah."

After that they walked in silence to one of the cane-fields. This field, like many of the others, was on a hillside. There were men there who were cutting the cane with machetes. The men who carried the cane collected the stalks and tied them into bundles. Ossie had no string, so he went to a nearby banana field and used his pen-knife to cut two dry strips of banana bark. He also cut off a dry banana leaf to be coiled into a cotta for his head. Then he returned to the cane-field, collected cane, and tied his bundle.

The next problem was how to get the bundle onto his head. He was used to carrying bundles of wood this way, but the bundle of cane was larger and heavier than wood. He observed how the men knelt with one knee against the hillside and, holding the cotta onto the bundle with their thumbs, then gradually eased the bundle over onto their right shoulders, and from there onto their heads.

Maas Eric was watching Ossie and he said, "You want me to help you up?"

"No, sah. I can do it myself."

Ossie looked at the bundle and thought of his grandfather and the mill. He wanted to show the men that he too could lift heavy things. He knelt with one knee against the hillside, positioned the cotta, and then he tried easing the bundle over onto his right shoulder. But the bundle was heavier than he thought.

"Boy, mind you strain yourself," said one of the cane-cutters.

"Take out some," advised Maas Eric.

"Is all aright, sah," replied Ossie.

"Leave him alone," said another cane-cutter. "Let him find him right weight."

On his second attempt Ossie lifted the bundle of cane to his head. It was heavy, but he felt he could make it to the mill-yard. He made the trip successfully, but he had to admit that the bundle was too heavy. As the cane-cutter had suggested, he gradually found his right weight, and he joined the flow of men carrying cane to the mill-yard. He followed Maas Eric, not allowing him to make a single trip more than him. It was a good feeling, being part of the work of the mill.

Then it was lunch time. Lunch was served at Uncle Tony's house which was close to the mill. Ossie walked with the men to the house. Each worker went into the kitchen and was served his lunch. Then they sat either on the verandah of the house or on the logs in the yard.

Lunch was served by Miss Esmine, Uncle Tony's wife. She was a buxom, sepia-complexioned woman who treated everyone in a motherly way. When it was time to serve Ossie she said,

"Boy, I have to give you a big lunch today. I hear you moving cane like any big man."

She piled his plate with mackerel cooked in coconut milk, boiled green bananas, and chunks of yellow yam. Ossie sat on one of the logs in the yard and enjoyed his lunch.

Then Miss Esmine served mugs of fresh cane juice. The juice was seasoned with ginger and cooled by chunks of ice bought from the ice-truck that morning.

After the meal the men relaxed, smoked and chatted. Then it was back to the cane-fields. The pace slackened, but the flow of cane from the fields to the mill-yard continued until close to sunset. A few men were still working when Ossie left the cane-field. But he had his evening chores to complete before it was night.

As he approached the mill-yard with his final bundle, Ossie saw Uncle Tony standing at the corner of the mill-yard overlooking the boiling-house. He was tall and coffee-complexioned and he had a straight nose. He was wearing his usual felt hat and blue shirt and pants. He was puffing his pipe as he surveyed the work of the mill. He watched Ossie as he unloaded his bundle of cane, then he said, "You worked very hard today."

"Yes, sah."

Uncle Tony nodded as he puffed his pipe.

"Good," he said.

"Gone, Uncle Tony."

"Tell your mother and father howdy."

"Yes, sah."

Ossie began his journey home.

The following week Uncle Tony sent a message to Ossie saying he wanted to see him.

The next Saturday evening, after he had completed his chores, Ossie went to Uncle Tony's home. He found him sitting on a bench on the verandah, and cutting tobacco on a cutting-board he had on another bench in front of him.

"Good evening, Uncle Tony," said Ossie.

"Good evening, son."

Uncle Tony got up and went into the house. He returned with a large bamboo joint; the top of the bamboo joint was covered with brown paper which was tied in place by a slender strip of banana bark. Uncle Tony handed Ossie the bamboo joint and said, "This is for working so hard last week Saturday."

"Thanks," said Ossie.

He pulled off the paper cover and looked inside. The bamboo joint contained wet sugar. Ossie smiled with pleasure.

"Gone, Uncle Tony," he said, still smiling.

"All right, Ossie."

Ossie hurried home with his bamboo joint of wet sugar. He thought of all the nice things his mother would make with it. But this, he felt, would be the sweetest sugar he had ever tasted, for it was the sweet reward of his labour.

The Parakeets

Ossie was very aware of the birds around him. He heard woodpeckers rattling their beaks on the trunks of trees. He saw inseparable pairs of ground doves waddling up stony pathways. He heard pea-doves cooing in fields of corn and peas. He saw petcharies eating bird-peppers from the trees which grew beside the house in which he lived.

There were times when he envied the birds their freedom. They were free to fly through the air as they wished. They were free from the pressures of school and chores. He often wished that he, like the birds, could move with such freedom over the hills and the valleys. Then there was the beauty of the birds. They were the most colourful things he knew. No other blue object matched the deep blue of the blue quit. There was no green like the green of the doctor-bird. The yellow of the banana quit was unmatched in its purity.

He was also fascinated by their wildness. The birds looked untouched by human hands. This quality of untouched wildness set them apart from the world in which he lived.

Ossie often found himself yearning after the freedom, beauty and wildness of the birds. One evening Ossie and Brightly were on their way home from school. They both had their wheels rolling in front of them. Brightly's wheel was made from the inner rim of a tyre; Ossie's metal wheel was from the old gear-box of a truck. When they got to the culvert overlooking Maas Harry's property, Brightly stopped his wheel and beckoned to Ossie to stop.

"You see that guango tree?" said Brightly pointing to a tree below the road, "parakeets have a nest in it."

"Where?" asked Ossie as he stopped his wheel.

"In the duck-ants' nest."

"Really? How you know that?"

"I was down there the other day looking for rabbit feeding, and I saw some parakeets on the duck-ants' nest. They kept flying away and coming back, and I heard the sound of young birds squeaking. So I climbed the tree to look, and I saw the nest with the baby parakeets in it."

"I want to see them," said Ossie.

"Sure," said Brightly. "Come let me show you."

They hid their wheels and school bags under the culvert and went through the field of gungo peas down to the guango tree. Brightly began climbing the tree and Ossie followed him. They climbed up to the old duck-ants' nest. Brightly looked in the nest first and then went beyond it so that Ossie could look in as well. Ossie got to the nest and looked inside. There were four half-naked baby parakeets in the nest.

"This is the first time I am seeing young parakeets," said Ossie.

"It was my first time too," said Brightly. "It is a pity people don't eat parakeets. These would be tender and juicy."

"They will be pretty when they grow up," said Ossie. "They will have green feathers and blue streaks on their wings."

They returned to the culvert, took up their bags and wheels and resumed their journey. As they rolled their wheels along the road Ossie kept thinking about the parakeets. He was so excited to come in such close contact with birds, and he was wondering if there was anything he could do about them.

It was while he was in bed that night that the idea came to him. He could cover the duck-ants' nest with mesh wire. That would enable the parent birds to feed the baby birds, but the young parakeets would be unable to get away. The parent birds would feed them until they were fully grown. Then he and Brightly could keep the parakeets as pets.

Ossie was excited by the prospect of actually owning parakeets. This would bring the world of the birds closer to him. All the birds would no longer be living in the bushes; he would have birds actually living at his home.

The following day he told Brightly about his idea.

"You smart fi true, Ossie," laughed Brightly. "You smart fi true, boy."

"But we'll have to get Maas Harry's permission," said Ossie.

"Sure," said Brightly.

A few evenings later, while he was on his way to the tank to fetch water, Ossie met Maas Harry coming from his field. Maas Harry had a bundle of grass on his head.

"Good evening, Maas Harry," said Ossie.

"Good evening, Ossie."

Ossie asked Maas Harry for permission to trap the young parakeets on his guango tree.

"Sure," said Maas Harry. "When I was a boy I used to like catching birds."

The following morning Ossie and Brightly decided to leave their wheels behind and play ten-ten instead. They left the wheels at Ossie's home and then set off for school. They began playing the game as soon as they were on the main road. They stood side by side and Ossie threw his stone about ten yards up the road. Brightly tried to hit Ossie's stone with his. He missed. Ossie then hit Brightly's stone with his and scored the first ten points. As the winner it was Ossie's turn to throw again. They moved quickly along the road as they played, and they spoke to each other between throws. Their conversation soon got around to the parakeets, and Ossie told Brightly that Maas Harry had given them permission to trap the birds.

"Good," said Brightly. "Now we are all set. But where will we get mesh wire?"

"We have some at home," said Ossie. "I'll ask my father for a piece."

"And what are we going to do with the birds when they grow up?"

"I want to keep mine in a cage," said Ossie.

"I want to sell mine," said Brightly.

"Sell them? Who to?"

"To passing motorists. I know a boy who made plenty money selling birds to passing motorists."

"I would never dream of selling mine."

"When can we get the mesh wire?"

"I will try for tomorrow."

That evening after school Ossie approached his father about the mesh wire. His father was in the yard sharpening his machete. He had the point of the machete stuck into the trunk of an ackee tree, and he leaned against the wooden handle as he filed the edge of the machete.

"Papa," said Ossie, "may I cut off a piece of the mesh wire?"

"Which mesh wire?"

"From the old fence behind the kitchen."

"What for?"

Ossie told his father about the parakeets, and about his wish to build a bird cage.

His father thought about it for a while, and then he told him to go ahead.

"But don't use up all the mesh wire," his father added. "We may need some of it one of these days."

"Can I also take some nails from your tool-box?" asked Ossie.

"Yes," his father said as he turned the machete over so that he could file the other side of the edge. The following morning Ossie and Brightly hid the mesh wire and nails under the culvert. In the evening after school they climbed the guango tree and, using stone as a hammer, they nailed the mesh wire over the nest of parakeets.

In the days that followed they visited the nest often, and watched the baby parakeets as they grew.

One Saturday morning after breakfast Ossie told his mother about the parakeets. He was sitting on the step in front of the back door. His mother was washing dishes on the bamboo dresser beside the kitchen. She had her back to him.

"Why do you want to imprison those poor baby birds?" asked his mother after he told her what he had done.

"Because I like birds, and I would like to keep some of them."

"What do you like about birds?"

Ossie scatched his head, and he spoke slowly and thoughtfully as he gave her his answer.

"I like their bright colours; and I like the fact that they can fly; and I like the wild look they have."

"These are the very reasons why you shouldn't cage them."

"What you mean, ma'am?"

"No caged parakeet will ever look as beautiful as a free one, and the poor birds won't be able to fly in the cage; and the caged birds will no longer have a wild look."

Ossie was silent as he tried to think of something to say.

"So if you really like birds," his mother continued, "you ought to let them go."

"But it is because I like them why I want to keep them," Ossie argued.

"You won't lose them if you let them go," said his mother.

"What do you mean?" asked Ossie.

"You can still enjoy them if they are flying free."

During the days that followed, Ossie thought about his mother's arguments. And he gradually came to the view that she was right. One evening he went alone to the guango tree and removed the mesh wire. When he went back a few days later the birds, now fully grown, were gone.

"Ossie, the parakeets gone!" exclaimed Brightly one morning at recess time.

"I know," said Ossie.

"You know?"

"Yes. I took away the mesh wire and set them free."

"What you do a thing like that for, man?"

"Because I prefer birds when they are free."

"You cause me to lose my money, man!"

"But it is better for the birds."

"Ossie, you are not a good businessman at all."

"Not when it comes to birds."

One Saturday evening, several weeks later, Ossie was on his way home from the bushes. He had a bundle of wood on his head. As he approached a bamboo clump which was beside the road he heard the screeching and chattering of parakeets. He stopped and looked and saw that there was a flock of parakeets in the bamboo clump.

As he stood and watched the parakeets, he noticed that one of them was giving him what seemed like a knowing look. It was possible, thought Ossie that the parakeets he had freed were now members of this flock. It was even possible that the bird looking at him now was one of those he had freed. He had no way of knowing. But he knew that he would never look at flocks of parakeets in the same way again. Each time he saw them he would remember the time he tried to trap part of their world and make it his own.

The flock of parakeets flew from the bamboo clump and began flying over the deep valley between Ossie and the distant hills.

Ossie watched as they flew away. The parakeets belonged to a world of freedom, beauty and wildness which he could still appreciate and enjoy, but which he had neither the right nor the power to try and own.

Fear of the Sea

efore that outing Ossie had never seen the sea. He had heard grown-ups talk about it, describing it as a big, deep thing made of water, which was sometimes very rough, and in which people caught fish. Those descriptions, however, did not tell him very much. Perhaps the best description he got was from an old man who said it was like the biggest field of cabbage one could imagine.

One year, a few weeks before Easter, a man named Maas Aston went around the district selling tickets for the three members of his family. Ossie had never been on an outing and he began to itch all over with excitement. During the days that followed, his parents had only to threaten not to take him along and he would rush to do anything they requested.

The day before the outing he got up early and completed all his chores. Then he bathed in the river which ran near their house. He regarded this river as an enormous quantity of water, and he found it hard to believe when people told him that compared with the sea it was almost nothing. They said it was just one of the hundreds of little rivers which flowed into the big rivers which in turn flowed into the sea. Ossie wondered about this strange thing which they said was like the sky but made of water, which had the colour of the mountains but was flat and rolling, and which was so irresistible people paid to visit it time and again.

Near sunset he went to the square to see what was happening there. The truck in which they would be travelling had already returned from its daily trip to Kingston, and it was now parked at its usual spot beside the wooded two-storey building at the northern end of the square. One of the sidemen was washing the cab, and two others were bent over the spare tyre pumping air into it. Some of the people in the square stood around the sidemen and watched; others were moving in and out of the shops in haste, before going home to prepare food for the trip.

Ossie left the square at dusk and began running home. His feet were light with anticipation as he ran. He swung around a bend and crashed into Adassa.

"Boy, why you don't look where you going?" she shouted angrily shoving him away.

In the half-light he noticed that her normally pretty face was contorted with anger, an anger too deep to be entirely the result of his bumping into her.

"Sorry, ma'am," said Ossie.

"Cho!" she said as she brushed past him.

"I didn't see you," he called after her.

She didn't answer and the grey form of her dress and head-tie quickly disappeared around the bend.

A little further down the road he saw Caswell, Adassa's boyfriend, sitting on a bank with his head and hands bent over his knees. Ossie said "Good evening" as he passed, but Caswell did not answer.

At home Ossie's mother and one of his aunts were in the kitchen preparing food for the outing. He went into the house and sat by the window where he could smell the fried chicken and rice and peas, and where he could listen to the women's voices while he watched the flickering of the fire behind the rows of bamboo wattling.

He slept lightly that night waking at the slightest sound, and he interpreted every crowing of a cock as a sign of daylight. When it was finally daybreak he was sleeping soundly and had to be awakened. It was still dark outside, but his parents had surer ears and noses for the sounds and smells of morning than he had.

They got dressed, and had breakfast. Then they set off for the square. They had the food in a bamboo basket with a lid, and they took turns in carrying it up the hill.

The square was full of colourfully dressed people who were greeting each other, chatting and laughing. The truck was now out on the main road between two of the shops; the back-board was lowered and people were climbing in. They were also climbing in through the side-door on the left. Ossie's mother and father climbed in through here too, and he left them to join in the scramble for a seat on the back row. These seats were in great demand since you got a better view from them. Ossie managed to squeeze in between two of his friends. There was a space in the middle to let people through, and one of the sidemen asked that it be saved for him. Ossie settled down comfortably and waited for the trip to begin.

Neville, the driver of the truck, lived in a rented room on the top storey of the wooden building. A few minutes later, he and Adassa appeared at the top of the outside stairway. Adassa was wearing a tight-fitting red dress, and her thick hair was combed back with only a few plaits and pins to keep it in place. Her face was fixed in a defiant smile, and she kept close to Neville as they walked down the stairway.

The image of Caswell sitting alone on the bank came back to Ossie, and he tried to remember if he had seen him since arriving at the square. Ossie stood up and looked around the square, then inside the truck. Caswell was sitting in the right-hand corner four rows away, watching the square through the space between the wooden bars at his eye level. He seemed to be staring vacantly, without focusing on anything or anyone in particular. Ossie turned and noticed that Neville and Adassa were about to walk along the right side of the truck. He remained standing to see if Caswell would react to them, and he did. When they came into his view, his body shook. Then he turned away from them and pretended to be watching the sidemen who were now collecting baskets over the wings of the truck. He turned again and, with bowed head and drooping shoulders, stared at the floor of the truck. Most of the passengers were chatting and laughing, but Caswell was the loneliest person Ossie had ever seen.

Then everyone could hear Neville and Maas Aston having an argument outside.

"I want mi wife and myself to drive in the cab," said Maas Aston. "Is me in charge of this trip."

"Is only Adassa I want inside there with me," said Neville. "If I don't drive oonuh can't go."

When people saw Maas Aston and his wife coming through the side-door they knew that Neville had had his way.

Maas Aston stood in front and counted the passengers. He ordered the sidemen to pull up the back-board. Then he reached over the wings and pulled the cord attached to the bicycle bell close to the driver's seat. The truck started and people began waving to those who were staying behind. Some watched with obvious envy, while others showered them with so many blessings and good wishes it was as if they were leaving for a foreign country.

The truck stopped a few times to pick up additional passengers. Soon they were out on the open road. Conversation slackened and they began singing. They sang 'Roll Jordan Roll' and 'Chi-Chi Bud O'. When they began driving on asphalted road they broke into the gear-box song:

Maas Aston:	Mr. Driver!
Passengers:	Drop in a gear for me.
Maas Aston:	Mr. Driver!
Passengers:	Drop in a gear for me.
	For when you are driving
	Remember your gear-box
	Drop in a gear for me.

Neville was famous for being a sweet-foot driver and, at the end of each round of the song, he changed gears with so much music and rhythm the people shouted with pleasure. He also tapped out the rhythm of the song on his horn.

Later they drove past enormous cane-fields, and large pastures in which herds of cattle grazed. They drove beside a large river, the size of which began to open Ossie's eyes to what the grown-ups had said about rivers and the sea. Then they began climbing into hilly territory. Ossie noticed the many small and thickly forested hills which were so different from the large mountains he was accustomed to seeing.

Ossie never forgot his first sight of the sea. Suddenly an enormous stretch of deep indigo hit his eyes; it seemed as if it had risen up suddenly out of the earth, before it fell again. People rushed to the wings. "The sea, the sea!" they shouted. "Look at the sea!" The truck turned away and the wide expanse of blue quickly shrank to a long strip before being swallowed up into the vegetation. Ossie found that his heart was pounding, that he was breathing heavily, and that his palms were moist.

For several minutes the sea seemed to be playing hide-and-seek with them.

Sometimes they were so close to it they could see the white spots that people in the truck said were waves. The next time they saw it, it was a mere strip of blue in the distance. It took some time for Ossie to realize that they were seeing the same sea from different directions as they followed the winding road along the coast.

Suddenly they were right up beside the sea, separated from it only by a concrete wall. Ossie looked out at the vast expanse of blue-green water, and felt nostalgia for the friendly intimacy of his little village stream. Now he could see the waves crashing against the wall, and he could hear the sea breathing and panting as if it were alive. They drove in silence as if it were irreverent to laugh and sing in the presence of the awesome being beside them.

After a few minutes they turned into a side entrance, and drove though a colonnade of coconut trees until they came to an open area where a number of vehicles, including a bus and a truck, were parked. At the far end of the open area Ossie could see a strip of white sand; beside it the sea lay quietly as if it had suddenly fallen asleep.

There were three buildings beside the beach: two thatched huts which were used as dressing-rooms, and a large club-house, also thatched, which contained a restaurant, a bar, and a place for dancing. The beach was already crowded with people from the other vehicles. There were also a few tourists with cameras. Some of the tourists had a motor-boat and were taking turns going out into the sea and coming back.

Most of the members of Maas Aston's party assembled in families and began eating. Later, a few changed into swimsuits and went into the sea. Very few of them could swim, so they splashed around at the edge of the water or sat on the sand. As soon as they had finished eating, most of the men headed for the bar.

Ossie did not go into the water; he had no swimsuit and he could not swim. He also felt a growing fear of the sea. So he walked along the shore with his friends and collected shells and driftwood.

Later in the afternoon a wind started blowing, and Ossie noticed the increased intensity of the waves. He heard a man telling listeners that the waves had the power to pull you in, and if they did, they would bring you back to the shore twice, but after the third pull you would be gone forever.

When they were tired of the beach, Ossie and his friends went into the club-house. There was a juke-box and people were dancing. Neville and Adassa were by themselves in a corner, close-dancing. Neville had a bottle of beer in his left hand and he hugged Adassa with his right. Their cheeks were pressed together as they danced.

After watching the dancers for a few minutes, Ossie and his friends turned their attention to the juke-box. They were admiring the way the juke-box changed records, when they heard the sound of someone screaming outside. The screams got closer and a woman rushed into the club-house.

"Caswell drownin'!" she cried. "Caswell drownin'!"

People stopped dancing and rushed out of the club-house. Ossie and his friends followed. The beach was lined with people who were all looking out into the sea.

When Ossie and his friends got to the front they saw a tall black man coming towards the shore with Caswell's body slung sideways across his shoulder. The man lay Caswell's body face-down on the sand. Caswell was wearing only striped underpants.

One of the tourists, a middle-aged woman with red hair, went forward and knelt beside his body. She rested her palms on his back and, putting her weight on them, began moving forward and backward as she tried to squeeze the water from his body. Each time she pressed forward, water sprouted from his nose and mouth. The woman who had taken the news to the club-house began describing what she had seen.

"I noticed that he wasn't lookin' too happy since mornin'. But is not my business what goin' on. Everybody can see what goin' on between Adassa and Neville. That is their business. But when I saw Caswell goin' into the sea I thought he was just going in to bathe. It didn't occur to me at the time that he might have something else on his mind. Then a little later I looked out and didn't see him any more. Then I spread the alarm."

A few minutes later the tourist got to her feet with a dejected look on her face. "I'm sorry," she said. "I've done everything I can. I'm very sorry, but he's dead."

The woman began wailing. "Look at the news we goin' 'ave to carry back! Look at the news we goin' 'ave to carry back to his parents!"

The tourists hitched their boat to their car and prepared to leave. The man who had taken Caswell's body from the sea asked them to report the death to the nearest police station. Most of the people began heading towards their vehicles. A number of vehicles left the beach. The people who had come in the bus had to wait; the man who had taken Caswell from the sea was a member of their party and he would be required to give a statement to the police.

As Ossie walked back to the truck he noticed that Neville and Adassa were sitting in the cab. Neville's eyes were red and he was pulling hard at a cigarette and inhaling deeply. Adassa was leaning back in her seat, her face cold and expressionless.

It was almost dusk when the police finally arrived. Ossie did not want to see what they were doing so he remained in his seat at the back of the truck. It was getting uncomfortably cold. Finally he heard the bus and the police van leaving the beach. The members of their party who had watched the examination and removal of the body began climbing into the truck. Soon afterwards the truck began retracing its path through the colonnade of coconut trees.

As they drove along the coast Ossie had his final glimpse of the sea, the sea that had taken Caswell. He glimpsed sections of its sad and immense loneliness. Each time he saw it he shivered at the thought of its unimaginable depths. He heard its panting as it intimidated the shore. Again, their truck kept moving first closer then away from it; gradually it merged into the encapsulating darkness.

They drove in silence for many miles. Then they began to sing. The truck became a wake on wheels. For Ossie the songs were as sad as his memory of the sea. And every time he thought of the sea, he felt a cold fear approaching his heart.

Glossary

Balm-yard:	A ritual site where a traditional form of folk healing is practised. Balmists combine the use of herbal and other remedies with a form of worship which includes drumming, singing, dancing and trance-like states.
Banana Day:	The day when bananas used to be taken by trucks to the coast to be loaded on to ships.
Bissy :	A drink made from the kola nut.
Cotta:	A circular pad placed on the head to protect it while carrying loads.
Gig:	A top which children play with.
Gizzadas:	Open tarts made of pastry and grated, sweetened coconut.
Higglers:	Pedlars, mostly women, who buy produce from farmers and sell it in markets, in cities or towns.
Mento:	A type of Jamaican folk music which uses $2/4$ rhythm, often has topical and humorous lyrics, and is accompanied by a particular form of dance.
Merino:	A knitted, usually sleeveless undershirt.
Mortar:	A vessel made by hollowing out a tree trunk in which produce or foodstuffs are pounded with a pestle.
Sweetcup whistle:	A whistle made from the sweetcup fruit.

Sweetfoot: A driver who gets musical sounds from his vehicle, especially by his use of the clutch and the accelerator.

Oonuh: You (plural).

Questions & Activities

Front Cover

1) What does the image on the cover say to you?
2) What kind of work does the person do?
3) What is the tool in the person's hand?

Bobbing Jones

QUESTIONS

1) If someone harms you, how should you respond? Tit for tat? Forgive the person? Report the offender to the authorities? Other? Defend your choice.
2) Should children be encouraged to make their own toys, or is it better to buy them from stores?
3) Farm theft, also called praedial larceny, is one of Jamaica's major problems. What do you think the country should do about it?
4) Dudley has both admirable and deplorable qualities. Identify and discuss them.
5) Some of the members of the community wanted Dudley to be killed by what is called 'vigilantism'. What are your views on this practice?

ACTIVITIES

1) Have a class debate the moot: "Punishment is useless unless it leads to reform".
2) Compose a song with the title, "Bobbing Jones Say".
3) Write an essay on the topic, "My Favourite Toy".
4) Some toys can be dangerous. What can increase safety in the use of toys?
5) Discuss a story or a film about toys.

A Voting Man

QUESTIONS

1) Should persons be harmed because they support a political party you do not like? Discuss this question.
2) Which do you think is better? Voting for the better political candidate or the better party?
3) Are the religious beliefs of a political candidate important? Defend your view.
4) Do you agree with Ossie's father's attitude to voting? Why should people vote?
5) What does the story say about the 'political education' Ossie is receiving?

ACTIVITIES

1) Compile a scrapbook on the topic: "How did Jamaicans achieve the right to vote?"
2) Have a class debate the topic: "Civics should be a compulsory subject in schools".
3) Write essays on the contributions of Jamaican leaders to the country. You may write on any leader you happen to admire.
4) Write an essay on the following topic: "How I came to know the things I know about Jamaican politics".

The Bamboo Fife

QUESTIONS

1) Did you guess correctly who the fife-player was? What led you to this conclusion?
2) Are duppies real or are they imaginary beings? Give reasons for your belief.
3) Why did schools have an Inspection Day? Ask your parents or older relatives to share their recollections of them with you.
4) Where did Ossie learn his songs? Where do you learn your songs? Is your musical education different from Ossie's?

ACTIVITIES

1) Have a class debate the moot: "Music is an important part of a person's education".
2) Can you play a musical instrument? Write an essay on how you acquired this skill.
3) Compile a scrapbook on Jamaican Mento music.
4) Write poems or paint pictures while listening to a recording of Mento music.
5) Invite a Mento musician to visit your class and talk about his music and his life.

Cricket Season

QUESTIONS

1) Cricket seems to be of great importance to West Indians. Why do you think this is so? Ask older relatives to tell you about cricket in their time.
2) Ossie saved his money in a bamboo joint. How do you save yours? Is your method safer than his?

3) Have you, or anyone you know very well, ever had possessions stolen? How does this make people feel?

4) What do you like or do not like about cricket?

5) Discuss the role played by each of the following characters in the development of the story: Ossie, Uncle Basil, Ossie's father, Vincent, the thief.

ACTIVITIES

1) Debate the following moot: "Every student should be encouraged to participate in at least one sport".

2) Write an essay on the topic: "The Game I Love Best", or "Why I Do Not Love Any Games At All".

3) Compile a scrapbook on the topic, "Great West Indian Cricketers".

4) Describe a cricket match you have played in or watched, as a short story.

5) Read poems about cricket, e.g. Egbert Moore's (Lord Beginner) "Victory Calypso, Lord's 1950", Benjamin Zephaniah's "How's Dat" or Ian Dieffenthaler's "Weather Report (for Chris Gayle)".

Brother Paul

QUESTIONS

1) Why do you think Ossie's mother did not want him to tell anyone about her sending him to the healer?

2) Do you think nutritionists would approve of the healer's recommended diet?

3) What are Ossie's mother's reasons for admiring the healer? Do you think they are good reasons?

4) Can our minds help us heal? Give reasons for your view.

5) Is there anyone like Brother Paul in your community? If so what are people's attitudes to him?

ACTIVITIES

1) Compile a scrapbook titled "Revivalism in Jamaica".
2) Listen to, sing, and discuss some Revivalist songs, e.g. "What a Wonderful Thing"' and Pukumina and Zion choruses.
3) View and discuss images of Revivalism e.g. their table, dress, musical instruments and wheeling dance.
4) View and discuss paintings that portray aspects of Revivalism, e.g. Albert Huie's "Mount of Prayer", Kapo's "Watching over me", and Osmond Watson's "Hallelujah".
5) Write poems or stories, or paint pictures, depicting your experiences or perceptions of Revivalism.

Admission: Children Ten Cents

QUESTIONS

1) The film show did not start at a set time. Why do you think this was so? Is this a good or bad thing?
2) Ossie succumbed to what is called 'peer-pressure'. Why do you think he did so?
3) Phonso was the ringleader of this escapade. Do you know anyone like him?
4) Ossie had reasons for putting seven cents into the collection plate. What are they? Do you think he constructed a good argument?
5) Are film shows put on in your community? How are they similar to or different from the one depicted in this story?

ACTIVITIES

1) Did the boys do something wrong by entering the church without paying? Write an imaginary essay from the point of view of Ossie or Phonso giving their views on this question.

2) Find out when and why Jamaica started using dollars instead of pounds.

3) Write a review of a religious film that you have seen on television or in a cinema.

4) Have you ever been pressured by other children to do something you did not feel like doing? Write a story about your experience.

5) Identify some of the chores that Ossie is required to do at home. Should children be required to do chores? Give reasons for your opinion.

Baptism

QUESTIONS

1) In this story Ossie learns things by listening to others as well as from his own experience. Identify the two and compare and discuss them.

2) Ossie could not recall ever seeing Miss Daphne looking at him. Yet at the baptism she appeared to recognize him. Have you ever been surprised to discover that someone knew you better than you thought he/she did?

3) Why is Ossie afraid of baptism? Is he likely to also have difficulty learning how to swim?

ACTIVITIES

1) Identify the different Christian denominations in Jamaica, and examine how each has contributed to the country's development.

2) Identify the major religions in Jamaica. Write a brief history of one of them.

3) Water is said to be a universal religious symbol. What is a symbol, and why do you think water is used as such an important example of it?

4) Do you think that converting from one religion to another is a right that all human beings should have? Write an essay defending your answer to this question.

The Sexton

QUESTIONS

1) Maas Rashie told Ossie to fear the living but not the dead. Why do you think he said that? Do you agree with him?

2) What does Jonas' cursing tell us about language and the meanings of words?

3) Why do you think Ossie helped Jonas get out of the pit? Why was he embarrassed when he was praised for doing so?

4) Ossie believed that it was funerals that made death a sad condition. Do you agree?

5) Sometimes the things people fear most happen to them (this is an issue, for example, in the Book of Job in the Bible). Was Ossie's experience with the goats an example of this?

ACTIVITIES

1) What do we owe the elderly? Discuss this issue.

2) Write a description of one of the elderly persons in your community.

The Kite

QUESTIONS

1) Stonebreakers are seldom seen today. Why do you think this is so?

2) Why do you think the stonebreaker is so fond of watching kites fly?

3) How do we know that Ossie enjoys making and flying kites?

4) Comment on Ossie's experience of bullying. Is bullying a problem in your school? What do you think should be done about it?

5) What lessons do Ossie and Lloyd Perry learn from Mrs. Annabella Nelson?

ACTIVITIES

1) Comment on this quote from the story: "There is nothing uglier than a kite with razor blades on its tail."

2) Examine this statement: "All bullies are cowards." Is this statement applicable to this story?

3) Organize a visit to, and/or participate in a kite-flying festival.

4) Is kite-flying a practice in your community? Write an essay about it.

5) Kites used to be weapons of war in ancient China. Make a scrapbook on the history of kites.

Ripe Bananas

QUESTIONS

1) Ossie believes that boys should not sell ripe bananas. Why does he believe this? Do you agree with him?

2) Did you learn anything new about Gros Michel bananas from this story? Can you recognize these bananas when you see them? How are they different from other bananas?
3) Do you think Mr. Llewellyn is a good teacher? Give reasons for your opinion.
4) Were you surprised by the school's response to Ossie's banana-selling? Why or why not?
5) The experience depicted in the story taught Ossie a number of things about his parents. What are they?

ACTIVITIES
1) Make a scrapbook on the history of the banana industry in Jamaica.
2) Read poems about bananas, e.g. Evan Jones', "Song of a Banana Man".
3) Sing songs about bananas, e.g. Harry Belafonte's "Day O" and the folksong "Banana".
4) Compile a list of food items made from bananas.
5) Write a story about the role played by bananas in your life.

Mango Ridge

QUESTIONS
1) Why was Ossie finding school such a difficult place?
2) Was Ossie a truant, or did he do the right thing?
3) As a result of his late sleeping, Ossie saw things in his home he had not noticed before. Identify them.
4) In Ossie's district the males bathed at a waterfall named Falling Waters. Where do you think the females bathed?
5) Ossie had a favourite spot on the land his parents owned. Do you have a favourite spot at your home? If this is so tell the class about it.

ACTIVITIES

1) Discuss the statement: "Schooling should be seen not only as a preparation for life but as part of life." Then write an essay on the topic from Ossie's point of view.

2) Make a scrapbook on the life of bees. Include a comparison of the facts with the bees-man's story.

3) Describe Nenen's description of how the world appears to someone who is hearing-impaired. Invite someone to translate her words into sign language for the class. Make this an opportunity to learn about this language.

4) Identify a proverb or saying that summarizes Ossie's experience of Mango Ridge and Clifton, his home district.

5) Describe what the story says about all the main characters in the story: Ossie, Ossie's mother, the bees-man, Nenen, Syl and 'Razor'.

The Reading Tree

QUESTIONS

1) Do you have a favourite reading spot? How is it similar or different from Ossie's?

2) Ossie chose a topic of much personal interest for his composition/ essay. Should students be encouraged to write on more essay topics like that?

3) Discuss the following quote from the story: "That tree is a tree of knowledge to the boy," said Teacher Llewellyn. Examine it as an example of a biblical allusion.

4) According to Mr Llewellyn, "The boy is writing well. And he is writing well because he is reading well." Why do you think he said this?

ACTIVITIES

1) Participate in the National Reading Competition.
2) Become members of libraries.
3) Form a book club.
4) Compile a list of quotes about the importance of reading (use the Internet).
5) It is said that the habit of reading is declining in the contemporary world. It is even said that there are now more writers than readers. What do you think are the reasons for these beliefs? And why are educators worried about these developments? Should they be?

Wet Sugar

QUESTIONS

1) The story describes how sugar used to be made in rural Jamaican districts. Did you learn anything new from it?
2) Why was 'Hercules' admired? Is there anyone like him in your community? Learn more about the Hercules of Greek mythology.
3) Ossie learns things from the men at the sugar-mill. What are some of the things he knows at the end of the story that he did not know at the beginning?
4) Ossie felt that the wet-sugar tasted even better because he helped to produce it. Have you ever had a similar experience?

ACTIVITIES

1) Make a scrapbook on the history of the sugar industry in Jamaica.
2) Have you ever seen or eaten wet-sugar? It is said to contain ash, sugars, phosphorus, calcium, potassium and sodium. How do its ingredients compare with counter and granulated sugar?

3) Many nutritionists say sugar can be harmful to health. Find out why they believe this. But can it be also good for health in some respects?
4) Arrange a field trip to a sugar estate.

The Parakeets

QUESTIONS

1) There are changes in Ossie's thoughts about birds as the story develops. Identify some of the causes of this change. Have you ever had a change of mind about something similar to Ossie's?
2) The story also describes some of the games and pastimes of boys in rural Jamaica. Are they similar to or different from yours today?
3) What are some of the things about Jamaican country life that you can learn from this story?
4) Ossie is clearly fascinated by birds. Which animals fascinate you most?
5) The characters in the story have different attitudes to birds. Examine each attitude.

ACTIVITIES

1) Compile a scrapbook on Jamaican birds.
2) Find out: a) which birds are endemic to Jamaica and
b) which are migratory.
3) Examine these questions: Are birds important for the environment? How can they affect human life? Invite an ornithologist to talk to the class about these questions.
4) Inquire into birdwatching as one of Jamaica's tourist attractions. Arrange a visit to Lisa Salmon's bird sanctuary in Anchovy, St James.

Fear Of The Sea

QUESTIONS

1) Describe Ossie's beliefs about the sea before he actually sees it.

2) Do you remember the first time you saw the sea? What did it make you feel and think?

3) What does the story tell us about Ossie's parents, Maas Aston, Caswell, Adassa, Neville and the unnamed tourist?

4) Did Caswell commit suicide? What reasons, if any, do we have for believing this?

5) Outings seem to be an important part of the life of Ossie's community. Is this also true of yours? If it isn't why do you think your community is different from Ossie's?

ACTIVITIES

1) Sing the songs that the holiday-makers sing while travelling on the truck.

2) Imagine and tell the story from Caswell's point of view.

3) Newspaper stories about holiday-drowning appear from time to time. Read and discuss one of these reports. Has this ever happened to anyone in your community? How did this make people feel?

4) How could Ossie overcome his fear of the sea? Write an essay about a fear you would like to overcome, or one that you succeeded in overcoming.

About the Author

Earl McKenzie (also known as St. Hope Earl McKenzie), was born in Mt. Charles in the hills of St Andrew, Jamaica.

He was educated at Paisley Elementary School, Oberlin High School, Mico College, Alberta College of Art, Columbia University, and the University of British Columbia where he received a PhD in Philosophy.

He is a former head of the English Department at Church Teachers' College, Mandeville, and is retired from the University of the West Indies, Mona, where he taught philosophy.

He is the author of three collections of short stories, one novel, three volumes of poetry, one multi-genre book and two texts of academic philosophy. He has had five exhibitions of his paintings.

In 2000 he was awarded a Silver Musgrave Medal for outstanding merit in the field of literature. In 2011 he received a Mico University College 175th Anniversary Award for distinguished service.

www.ingramcontent.com/pod-product-compliance
Lightning Source LLC
Chambersburg PA
CBHW051925240626
47153CB00004B/1370